The Irish Captain

The Irish Captain

by P. J. Kavanagh

1979

Doubleday & Company, Inc., Garden City, New York

Previously published under the title of *Scarf Jack*

Library of Congress Cataloging in Publication Data

Kavanagh, Patrick Joseph Gregory, 1931–
The Irish captain.

First published in 1978 under title: Scarf Jack.
I. Title.
PZ4.K218Ir   1979   [PR6061.A9]   823′.9′14
ISBN: 0-385-13684-6
Library of Congress Catalog Card Number 77-25599
Copyright © 1978 by P. J. Kavanagh
All Rights Reserved
Printed in the United States of America
First Edition in the United States of America

For Cornelius and Bruno

CONTENTS

The Irish Militia are totally without discipline, contemptible before the enemy when any serious resistance is made to them, but ferocious and cruel in the extreme when any poor wretches either with or without arms come within their power; in short, murder appears to be their pastime.

Lord Cornwallis,
Commander-in-Chief in Ireland
1798

I was directed by the smoke and flames of burning houses, and by the dead bodies of boys and old men slain by the Ancient Britons, though no opposition had been given to them and, as I shall answer to Almighty God, I believe a single gun was not fired, but by the Britons or Yeomanry. I declare there was nothing to fire at, old women, and children excepted. From ten to twenty were killed outright; many wounded, and eight houses burned.

John Giffard,
Protestant, Captain of Dublin Militia

The Irish Captain

The Hanged Man

The story begins on a winter's afternoon in Gloucestershire, not long after Christmas. All the previous summer there had been a terrible rebellion in Ireland. My mother said she thought it was a revolt of Catholic peasants against their harsh Protestant landlords, but others feared the French might take advantage of the troubles, invade Ireland and with Irish Catholic support invade us. Mr. Hicks, down on the plain in Cheltenham, had begun to raise a militia of gentleman-volunteers, and other recruits, in order to protect us should this happen and the regular Army be too busy elsewhere. It was a troubled and fearful time, even in our small village.

On this particular afternoon I was making my way home as usual through the woods, walking from the manor where I took my lessons with my cousins, to the small cottage where I lived alone with my mother. My father was Irish, which is why my mother knew so much of the conditions there, and had been an officer in the British Army, but he had left us many years before.

There was a storm coming, everything was very still. I had had a bad day with our tutor Mr. Turner so I promised myself that after supper I would slip away from the house before the storm broke and go down to the copse to see if there were rabbits in my snares. In this way I hoped to drive Mr. Turner from my mind.

I was not really allowed to set snares. My mother disapproved of me taking Mr. Edward's property, even though he was married to her cousin, but I could never believe that these wild things *were* his property, and the allowance he gave her to live on was not large enough for her to be able to refuse a rabbit she could put in her pot. She would give me a stare when I produced one, but as she turned away I always thought I could see her looking amused, and anyway, to tell the truth, I never managed to snare all that many. There were villagers who were up to the same game and they were better at it than I was.

So after I had eaten and talked with my mother for a while I went up to my room and climbed out of my window over the roof below and onto the bank behind our cottage. There were steps cut into this bank among the tall beech trees and these led up to our woodshed and then to the lane. I went into the shed first, because I always did, and because keeping our cottage supplied with wood was my task. I saw with satisfaction that there were plenty of split logs remaining, though I had carried a load down the day before, and that the kindling was dry under a sound patch in the somewhat ruined roof. Then, feeling a good husbandman, I crossed the lane and entered the field that fell away on the other side of it, where, in the copse, lay my snares.

It was growing dusk by this time, but I did not mind that. I loved to be out in the dark and was proud of the way I could move about in it, telling myself stories of adventure and making, or so I thought, hardly any noise. The storm still held off but it was going to be a big one, for there was an even greater stillness as though the evening held its breath. I knew I would have to be quick, for if my mother found that I was out of the house in a storm she would become anxious.

Then I thought I heard thunder: a strange, steady sort that made me stop in the field and listen. There came an even stranger noise, very unusual in that lonely spot at any time, the sound of voices. A company of horsemen was approaching! I turned back and hid in the hedge by the lane so that I could see who passed. Then the heavens opened as though they had been saving all their waters for just the spot where I lay. The horsemen were almost abreast of me by this time and they slowed as the rain hit them. The leader held up his hand as a signal for them to halt. I saw him clearly enough. He was a thin, shabbily dressed man with heavy eyebrows and black hair that straggled from under his hat and onto his collar. His horse steamed in the rain as though they had been riding hard and long.

"For the love of God, this looks as good a spot as any," came the voice of a man at the back whom I could not see. "Have we not come far enough, riding and hiding?"

He spoke in a strange singsong fashion I had not heard before.

The leader seemed uncertain; he sat still on his horse while the water bounced off his cape and flowed in streams from the brim of his hat. It also ran in rivers down the back of my neck but I dared not move.

Then he gave a grunt and dismounted in a shower of spray, saying in the same sort of voice, but harsher, "Ye're right for once! We can't be far off the place he mentioned. He said the middle of England so none could tell which coast the rat came from, and convenient to himself so he could see his friends had done the work. And that's us!" He gave a cruel laugh. "Let his friends get it over with then. I've been looking forward to it!"

By what light there was still in the sky I could see there were four of them, made big by thick caped coats, and among them was another horse on a leading rein with a huge pack tied to its back. They all dismounted and one of them made towards the burdened horse, clicking open what I took to be a knife. "No!" The leader shouted out to this man. "Untie the knots, you fool! We need the rope for the business! And we must get off the road; there's a gate along here." He was too late because the man had already slit through a rope that passed under the horse's belly and the huge pack slipped from the horse and slapped heavily onto the stones of the road, the man with the knife making no movement to prevent it. This was so near to where I lay that my face was splashed by the fall and I saw, clearly enough, that this was no pack but a man, trussed with cords. He lay with the side of his face on the rough lane and near enough for me to see in the dusk that his eyes were open and looking directly into mine. I shall never forget the expression in those eyes: they looked at

me as though a boy's face was the most natural thing to
see in a hedge when you lay yourself helpless in the mud.

Quickly I pulled my own face away. They were coming
into the field where I lay and I had no wish to be discovered by men like these. I scuttled, head down, towards
the copse in the middle of the field, before they could
come through the gate and see me, for the copse was the
only place where I could hide. I had seen enough to know
that these were savage men and I had heard enough also.
For when the leader had shouted at the man with the
knife for cutting the rope, telling him he should have
waited for his pleasure, the man had begged to be allowed to finish the business with his knife and slit the
prisoner's throat. "I tell you, no!" roared the leader—I
heard it even as I ran head down towards the trees, de-
voutly wishing I was at home with my mother—"No!" he
shouted, as though they were alone in the world, "we
were told to make him suffer as we make his beloved
rebels suffer and so I swore and so we shall!" and there
was a sort of cheer from the other ruffians and laughter.
They were right not to fear being overheard in the dark
in that weather but I thought if I was their captain I
would make them go about their business more silently.

They filed through the gate leading their horses, the
bound prisoner thrown again across the back of the rider-
less one with his feet trailing to the side of it, and they
made straight for the copse where I was hidden.

At the edge of the copse is a very ancient oak tree, half
its huge roots going back into the wood among the ashes
and elders, the other half going out into the field making
great humps in the neat sheep-cropped turf. It is so hollow inside you can stand up in it, but with only a small
hole by the roots on the copse side so that I knew I could

wriggle into it but I doubted if a grown man could. I squeezed inside it as quickly as I could, my haste and my wet clothes making me for one moment fear that I was stuck fast, and once inside I said a desperate prayer that I should not be discovered for I now had no doubt what my fate would be if I was. But I thought my chances of safety were good. To look at the old oak you would never guess it was hollow; in summer it still put out plenty of leaves on its topmost branches and even its huge lower boughs, each of them thick as an ordinary tree, had sap and strength in them still.

So the leader seemed to judge, for through a knothole, keeping well back so there was no chance of my white face showing, I saw him step under the oak and appear to look up at it, and heard him say, "This will do us."

It was dark now and the rain was, if possible, worse. They were clearly impatient to be done. One of them, opening one side of his coat, made a tent for another man to strike a flint and light a masked lantern. "Will it not be seen?" said another man, anxiously, and the one who held it laughed. "If it is they'll think it's the fairies! . . . On a night like this? It's only fools like us are out in it. The Colonel'll be feasting by now in front of the fire at the manor. And his Captain."

They turned their attention to the prisoner, pushing him off the horse so that he fell again. They stood in a circle round him, the lantern making a small round glow in the long spikes of rain that hit the ground and splashed up, glinting.

Two of them stooped and hauled him up, supporting him. Their backs were to the tree so that I could just make out the prisoner's face, rain streaming down it, washing off the mud and a darker stain that I took to be blood caused by his falls.

The leader said, "We shall do it properly. You shall have no cause for complaint. Gentlemen, how do you find? Guilty or not guilty?" "Guilty!" said all the others, laughing, and the leader said, "D'ye see? . . . Anything to say?" The man with the lantern held it up to get a better look, the two men supporting him stood aside and the prisoner swayed as though he would fall, bound as he was, but he did not. He turned his head and looked each of them in the face slowly, as though memorizing their features. Then he shook his head.

His calmness seemed to infuriate them all, and the leader said, almost hissing, his face pressed up close to his, "By God, I'd like to prepare a pitch cap for you!"

"Aye, and a taste on the triangle," growled the one with the lantern.

"But the rain would put the pitch cap out," said the leader, "and we have no time. Nor, my Jack, have you. Make ready!" he shouted.

At this command the two men who had not spoken unwound the rope that was round the poor man's legs, tied it to the rope that had bound him to the horse, and one of them began to make a noose of one end while the other took the remaining part of the rope and began to climb the tree; he passed so near to my nose that I could smell the reek of his wet clothes. It was an easy tree to climb because its vast boughs stuck out regularly like a ladder, and once he was up there he passed the end of the rope, I supposed, over one of them. The man below was having difficulty making the noose—I heard him cursing the wet rope and heard the leader telling him to hurry—but at last he too was finished and I saw the noose thrust over the head of the condemned man. They pulled it so cruelly tight that he tottered. Then two men hoisted him onto the horse he had been tied to, called to the man up the tree to take the slack, and he was pulled from above until his feet were on the horse's back, his chin dreadfully forced up with the knot to the side of it. When they judged the rope was taut enough—it was clear they were practiced in this business—they called to the man up the tree to slacken it off a little. When this was done to their satisfaction the leader called out, "Make fast!" "Done!" came the call from the tree after a pause, during which the prisoner was supported upright on the horse by two men, and the leader stepped forward. "Good-by, Captain. I never enjoyed a night's work better!" and he gave the horse a tremendous thwack on the rump with the palm of his hand so that it lifted its head and jerked forward a few paces uncertainly, far enough to make the man fall the length of slack in the rope, stop with a sudden check and hang there swinging, his feet pointing straight down, his head at an angle.

The man with the lantern spat on the hanging man's coat, holding the light up to look at his face, shielding it from the rain with his arm. They stood there in a ring, rain running off their clothes, their faces becoming shadows and hollows, like skulls, as the man lowered his light. They were silent a moment as though struck with the suddenness of what they had done.

I knelt inside the oak and almost buried my face on the dry powdery stuff on the floor, sniffing its familiar smell for comfort, half-believing that if I hid my face I would make myself even more invisible.

I need not have feared. They clearly did not want to linger round their crime and the rain made them more than ever anxious to be gone. They climbed onto their horses, leading away with them the now unburdened packhorse, and quickly made their way in single file towards the gate more silently than they had come.

Before they left the field they moved out of my sight, so I waited a few moments until I could hear no sound but the rain. Then, cautiously, I put my head out of the base of the old oak and saw, as well as was possible in the teeming darkness, that the field was empty. With great difficulty I squeezed the rest of me out into the rain. It was as though my wet clothes had swollen on my body and for a moment I thought I might have to stay inside the tree until they dried, while the man swung on the end of his rope a few feet from me. I had a hope he might still be alive. The job had been done hastily, in the dark, and I had heard tales of men hanged who had lived on to old age and of other poor wretches who had survived the drop only to have to climb their gallows again to allow the executioner a second try.

As soon as I was out of the tree I ran to the side where he swung and climbed the branches behind him. I had a knife in my pocket that I used for splitting the pegs of my snares and I set to work on the rope above his head.

It was taut with his weight, and wet, so I had to saw at it, fearful my knife would blunt before the last strands snapped. The palm of my hand rubbed raw with the effort of it until at last, closing my eyes, I gave a last desperate saw to the hemp and the rope parted. My shut eyes could not prevent me hearing the sucking splash as the big body fell, helpless as a sack, to the ground below. When I looked down I saw he had sprawled half-forward, half-sideways, and I prayed the rain-soaked ground had made the drop easier for him, if he was still in this world.

He had hit the ground hard three times that night to my knowledge.

As fast as I could I was down and forced myself to look at his face. I turned it gently away from the mud, pushing at his shoulder so that in the end he toppled onto his back. It cost me much to do this because, if alive, his bones might be broken and I might be doing him a worse injury than any he had yet received. But I liked his face, which had seemed a peaceful one, and I could not bear to see it lying in the mud.

The knot of the rope stuck out from his windpipe like a cravat but because it was a noose I was able to loosen it with my fingers, with difficulty as it was wet, but in the end I managed it, and felt the terrible welt where it had bitten into the flesh.

There seemed no life in him, no breath, and I knelt on his chest to see if I could make the bellows of his lungs work. I could no longer worry about whether his ribs were broken, his neck or his back, for if he did not breathe soon he would have no use for any of them.

It was hard to know if I did any good, because although I was a large enough boy, my knees seemed very small on his huge thick coat and I could not feel his rib cage move. But perhaps what I did was useful or perhaps it was never necessary because to my great joy his lips parted and a moan came from between them. My friend (for so I already thought of him) had escaped his captors as somehow I had always felt in my bones that he would.

As I bent over him his eyes opened and I could just see him staring up at me as he had done before, calm as an animal.

"We have met before," he whispered, "on the road."

Then after a pause in which he gathered strength he said, "Gone?"

I took him to mean the men who strung him from the tree and I nodded, finding it difficult to speak. So did he, for he opened his mouth again and shut it, gasping.

I lifted his head and slipped the noose over it and then he rolled himself slowly on his side so that I could reach the ropes around his wrists which had shrunk so much that it was difficult to cut these without cutting his flesh; they had bitten into it almost as badly as the rope about his neck.

He suffered all this patiently and when he was at last free he rolled on his back again and lay looking up at me, unmoving.

If only I could now get some help! But my cousins at the manor were a mile away and would ask too many questions, perhaps would feel they ought to tell their father, and I could not risk that until I knew more about this man. There were cottages at the bottom of the field near the stream but none of the villagers could I trust either, at least until I knew more. And my mother was not to be thought of.

"Where are we?"

"Near the town of Gloucester, sir."

Without thinking I spoke like a country boy. Thought of my mother had reminded me that I did not want this man to know more of me than I did of him. Would he not expect me to take him home? This I dared not do.

He seemed pleased by my reply, as though this was the place he had expected to find himself. He nodded, or tried to, but winced. "I don't think I can stand, boy," he said.

Into my mind had already come a place I could take

him where he would be safe at least for a while, though whether long enough for him to recover his strength I did not know.

But I could not move him. With my hands under his armpits I pulled until blackness floated in front of my eyes but he barely moved an inch. He rolled on his face and tried to raise himself onto his knees but he sank down again at once.

When he was on his back again I pulled and he tried with his heels to push. Inches at a time he began to move, but his heels slipped on the mud and mine slipped from under me so that I was nearly as often flat in the mud as he was, with his back lying heavy on my legs.

The storm had passed over us and the rain had stopped. A light breeze had arisen and on it, freezing my blood, was borne once more the sound of approaching horses.

Then I heard wheels fighting their way through ruts, jingling harness and the cries of a coachman. It was a carriage being driven as fast as the state of the lane would allow; too fast, by the sound of it. A carriage was unknown on that lane, though it was indeed a short cut from the main turnpike road should any gentleman urgently wish to reach the manor. But why should anyone want to do that? And would they see us from their windows, two dark figures struggling in a field, or would the coachman on his high seat look down?

If I had pulled before to the limit of my strength I now pulled until I felt my arm sinews and my leg sinews crack and feared that my heart would burst entirely, as it seemed to do, for at that moment a huge hand was clapped over my mouth from behind and a word hissed in my ear. But before I could connect the word—which I knew was "Still!"—with any meaning, my senses left me and I felt myself falling backward into a darkness deeper than the darkness of the night.

2

Caleb Bawcombe

When I next opened my eyes I was propped in the corner of a place I recognized, though it was pitch-dark, by its smell. Then a tinder sparked and by the slowly growing light of a candle stub—one I had put in the hut myself—I saw a huge caped figure bent over the bunk unbuttoning the surcoat of the man I had tried to rescue.

He lay on his back on the bunk with his gentleman's boots sticking over the end of it. I had noticed the fineness of his clothes when I had tried to drag him to this place. Now I heard him groan and his teeth begin a dreadful clattering.

I must have made some noise as I came to myself, for

the man in the cape said quietly, without turning, "Help, boy, or we've a dead man."

For the first time that night I felt myself near tears. I realized I had been more full of terrors than I knew. When I heard that welcome voice a great burden was lifted from me and I was no longer alone. It was Caleb Bawcombe!

Caleb—famous throughout the county for his strength: stonewaller by day and poacher by night: oldest and largest of a formidable band of brothers.

I suppose I was still stupefied, still in a dream, for as I sat and stared and got my bearings, all that came into my mind was a picture, a memory of an incident I had watched months ago from the schoolroom window at the manor.

One morning I had seen Caleb standing on the terrace below, tenderly cradling a pup, for he was also a famous breeder of terriers. Mr. Edward was discussing the price of it with his servants. The contrast between the shabby, bearded Caleb and the thin elegance of Mr. Edward surrounded by the green swallow-tailed coats of his servants was striking. It seemed Mr. Edward was behaving with more than his usual coolness, for he hated Caleb whom he called The Torment and would dearly have liked to have him clapped in Gloucester jail, but there was no gamekeeper who dared lay a hand on Caleb in the woods. It was clear that the servants were imitating their master and were behaving with equal haughtiness. Caleb suffered this until it appeared that a price had been agreed whereupon he attempted to hand the pup, still cradled in both his arms, to Mr. Edward. But Mr. Edward made an impatient gesture and a servant took the dog by the scruff, holding it away from him, and handed Caleb some coins. Whereupon Mr. Edward turned on his heel and made to return to the house.

Caleb had remained standing there and despite the difference in their clothes and situation it seemed to me there was a grandness about Caleb. Then a daring servant, I suppose trying to impress his master, came a few steps towards Caleb, fluttering his hands at him and telling him to be off. Caleb suffered this too, merely looking at the servant who slowly lost confidence in his gestures and to my delight took a couple of paces backwards, quite out of countenance, and retreated to join his master who had turned to watch from the top of the terrace steps. Caleb continued to stand there for a moment or two, quite still, his hand still outstretched with the coins in the open palm. Then he too turned and walked slowly down the drive, and there was something royal about his lonely figure. Then there fell on my head the round ruler of Mr. Turner who began one of his lectures about my ingratitude for being given a gentleman's education when I was too idle to take advantage of it, and my cousins shuffled their feet at their desks because we had all heard it many times before.

Such was Caleb Bawcombe. A man who more than once had seen the inside of Gloucester jailhouse for the damage his fist had inflicted on some wretch who had dared to cross him. A man who spent half his life outside the law, with a string of stalwart brothers to support him, and who owed no love or loyalty to the powers by which he was surrounded. He was not the man to betray a fugitive, whatever the fugitive might have done. Indeed he was the one man who could help him. It was perhaps possible to save the hanged man after all!

"Boy!" The summons was urgent, and half in fear (for Caleb had no reason to love me) and half in gratefulness, shaking myself from my dream, I hastened to the side of the bed.

"Help me prop him." Together we got the man's coat off his shoulders. He was shuddering helplessly now, in a fever. "Lucky I was out, loosing a few of your snares, lad. You put too many." Caleb spoke quietly as he worked. We pulled off the man's boots, drawers, undershirt, all soaked with rain and sweat. Caleb wanted him entirely naked. "Make a fire, a hot one." He spoke harshly now, pushing me away, but not before I had seen the red and white weals of an old flogging across the man's back. "Here, drink this," I heard Caleb say, and as I knelt at the stove I saw him hold a small flask to the man's clashing teeth, supporting him while he drank. The man was shivering so violently that he could not keep still enough to drink and much of the liquor went down his chin. But some of it must have gone through his teeth, for I saw the dreadful shivering subside and he sank back on the cot. "Thank you," he said; the first words he had spoken since Caleb began ministering to him.

There was a large piece of sacking hung on two nails to cover the hut window. Over this, on the two nails, Caleb hung the man's enormous coat and as soon as it was fixed to his satisfaction and no light was showing he withdrew the sacking from beneath the coat and began to wrap the man carefully. "You'll be needing something to sweat into, friend." Then he said in a different voice, "How's the fire?"

I had laid in plenty of dry kindling, for this hut was a favorite place of mine, and when I had stuffed a pile of it inside the door of the little iron stove Caleb held the can-

dle flame to it and soon it took. When it began its small
crackling roar he shut the door of the stove and jerked his
head towards the pile of logs in the corner. "Those dry?"

"As bones, sir," I said and Caleb looked at me.

"We don't want no smoke from wet logs. Not bad for a
gentleman's son."

I felt the man on the bed watching us although our
backs were towards him, and I said to Caleb, in my country voice, "I come in here sometimes when I'm watching
sheep and the master would be angry with me if he saw
smoke."

Caleb paused in his placing of wet clothes round the
stove and turned to me. "Would he now?" he said. "Well,
you won't be telling your master of all this, I dare say. Or
your *mistress*," he went on, staring hard at me and meaning, I supposed, my mother. I shook my head.

I had not even told my mother of the existence of this
hut. It was on wheels, the kind shepherds use to take up
to high places in bad weather so that they can spend the
night with their flocks. It must have been broken in some
way for it had lain undisturbed in the copse for as long as
I could remember, overgrown with Old Man's Beard,
briars, and brambles, so that a near-passer would hardly
guess it was there, or mistake it for an old pile of fallen
wood. I thought I was the only one who knew of it, but of
course Caleb did, who was as much a part of these fields
as the badgers and the dog foxes I could hear from my
bed at night. When I thought of my bed I remembered
my mother again and wondered how I was going to explain my lateness.

Caleb arranged all the clothes round the fire, which
was now giving out a good heat, as carefully as a house-
wife. When he was satisfied, he moved back to the bunk

and said gently to the man who lay quite still now, with the stillness of exhaustion but with those observing eyes always open, "You'll be having nothing to eat, I reckon." He reached under the cape that protected the shoulders of his huge flapping coat, once black but now with a greenish tinge of old age, and produced a crust of dark bread which the man accepted and began to bite, swallowing painfully. At the same moment Caleb stooped quickly forward, and from the sacking that surrounded the man he fished up with one finger a black cord that was round the man's neck, until, pulled through the sacking, there appeared a small ornamental cross that glittered in the candle flame.

"They left you this then?"

For the first time I thought I detected anxiety in the man's face. He stared up at Caleb and I felt if he had had the strength he would have hurled Caleb against the wall rather than lose his cross. I myself was unsure whether Caleb would put it in his pocket, for I had all my life heard nothing but bad of him, and perhaps after all it was only my silliness that made me admire him. Caleb looked at the cross as though unable to make up his own mind; then he carefully put it back under the sacking against the man's breast.

"You run off along home now, lad," he said to me. "I'll stay here until these clothes be dry." He looked at the clothes with satisfaction, for they were all now comfortably steaming and the hut itself had become extremely hot. "We can't have a fine gentleman like this spending the night in sackcloth."

The man made to speak but Caleb stopped him, producing once more the miraculous flask. The man drank greedily, taking it from him and tipping it so that I heard the neck of it gurgle. "There's more where that came from," said Caleb and for the first time the man smiled a frank smile, or perhaps it was a reckless one, for certainly he had no more to lose, unless it were that cross. If Caleb cut his throat he would be no worse off than he had expected to be not an hour before. Then he began to speak, still hoarse but in a lilting way, like the ruffians who had tried to hang him but less so. "You would have tied the knot better, I'm sure," he said. "You'd think they'd had enough practice hanging men."

"And where would they get such practice?" said Caleb.

"In Ireland," said the man. "Where else?"

"You come from Ireland then?" said Caleb.

"I do. And am no fine gentleman either. Or no finer than the gentlemen into whose hands I am fallen."

"I never heard of a gentleman being flogged," said Caleb, thoughtful.

"You see?" said the man, giving us both a crooked smile. But the speech, and the attempt at charming us— for so I saw it was—had tired him and he lay back, looking at us, seeming relaxed and easy in the knowledge that Caleb had him at his mercy.

"Cut along with you, boy," said Caleb. "Can you be here in the morning? Bring some food if you can but don't alarm your mother now. Wait! I'll shield the light!"

"A carriage . . . Did I not hear one? . . . You carried me," said the man.

"Ah. You did. And I did."

The man on the bunk smiled faintly. "He'll be here then, to see me swinging. That rope. Move it . . . if you would be so kind."

"*I'll* do that," whispered Caleb to me, holding the door open, shielding the candle under his cape. He stopped me as I made to leave, holding my arm hard. "No word of this at the big house," he muttered. Then, as though the words cost him an effort, "You did well though." With that he had me through the door so fast that the brambles covering the entrance to the hut caught and tore at my clothes, and I stood on the two little steps detaching them from my coat and pushing them back so no disturbance could be seen. Then, so quickly had he had me out of the door and the door shut behind me, it took me a moment to understand I was out in the dark field again with an almost impossible problem before me: how to explain my long absence to my mother and the fact that I was almost entirely coated in mud.

I clung to the dark edge of the field, where there was cover, for I had no wish to encounter that dreadful band again if they took it into their heads to return. And as I crept along the side of the lane I could find no solution to my difficulty except to tell my mother the whole truth. But I could not do that. The secret of the stranger's existence might be a dangerous one to know. The only hope was that my mother had fallen asleep in front of the fire, as she sometimes did, and so had not noticed my absence. I was doubtful about the chances of this, because the rainstorm had been an exceptionally fierce one and storms always made my mother restless.

However, yet another surprise was in store for me that night. When I slid down the bank and up the roof to my unlatched bedroom window, the house was unusually quiet. At the bottom of the stairs was a door to keep draughts out of the parlor, and there was no chink of light at the bottom of it. So with my boots in my hand I crept down the stairs, deciding my mother must have fallen asleep after all and the lamps had burned smoky.

But when I carefully opened the stairs door and looked into the parlor I saw at once that it was empty. I had been right. The house had been too quiet. There was no one in the house at all.

This alarmed me, it was so unusual. I could not remember that my mother had ever gone out at night without warning. Could those men have been here? I turned up the lamps which burned low as though my mother had left them on for her return, but there was no sign that any stranger had been in the room. Anyway, the last I had seen of the men they had clearly been determined to put as much distance between themselves and the man left hanging as they could.

So I put the mystery to the back of my mind and decided to make the best use of it that I could. I stripped off my clothes and wrapped myself in a rug like a red Indian. My clothes I set to dry in front of the fire which I stirred into a blaze. Then I scraped and washed my boots in the scullery, making sure to throw the dirty water out of the back door. The boots I set near the fire also, but not too near. Cracked boots were a serious matter. Though Mr. Edward gave us all the money he could so that we could support ourselves, my mother was often worried how to replace things that had been spoiled. A servant came each quarter with the money, and my mother signed a paper. Mr. Edward we seldom saw; he never came to our cottage.

I gave myself some cheese to eat and settled myself in my rug in front of the fire, waiting for my clothes to dry, reflecting how different my circumstances were from those of the poor wretch in the hut. I, in my own house, waiting for my mother to return. He, miles from home, dependent on what help he might get from a ruffianly looking stranger and a white-faced boy who swooned like a girl at a shock. Though, of course, I had only fainted from the effort of trying to drag him over the mud.

That mud was drying on my coat already and I reached into the pocket for my knife so that I could begin to scrape it off. My knife was not there. After cutting the man free I must have dropped it . . . "He'll be here. To see," the man had said. And I remembered his anxiety to have the rope taken down. My knife would be there if anyone came to that place and burned into the wooden handle with a poker were my initials . . .

I could not go back to get it. That effort was beyond me, at least until morning. I remembered the watchful resignation of the man in his bunk, content to do nothing about what could not be helped. I tried to be like that myself, but I kept thinking of my knife lying there, as broad as day. Who could miss seeing it?

But the devil himself would not have got me out of the house again that night. So I scraped with a kitchen knife, and so hot was the fire, so carefully did I toast first one side of my clothes then the other, that I was just deciding there was scarcely a stain to show of my adventure when I heard the pad of more than one pair of feet in the garden, and my mother's voice.

3

Captain Jack

I had time to put on my clothes before my mother came in. After she had exclaimed at the atmosphere in the parlor, which she said was like a washhouse, and heard my explanation, which was that I had been caught in the worst of the storm just near the house, she noticed that I steamed where I stood and bade me take my clothes off again and resume my Indian blanket; so I was soon back the way I was when I first heard her voice and footsteps. Fortunately she was still too flurried and excited to notice the remains of mud which, despite my scrapes with the kitchen knife, still clung to my coat and breeches.

It seemed that soon after I had gone out she had been

sent for by Mrs. Edward, her cousin. Mrs. Edward was the lady of the manor, married to the man who had taken on the expense of keeping myself and my mother.

Two men bearing a sedan chair, an antique style of transport sometimes used by Mrs. Edward who suffered from poor health, had arrived at our cottage door. My mother told me that Mrs. Edward had insisted on the chair because she wanted to see her immediately and because the skies threatened so darkly. I asked the names of the servants who had carried the chair and when my mother told me I could not help smiling: either Mr. Edward chose his servants because he detected in them a chilliness of manner which matched his own or they imitated their master, and these were two of the haughtiest. I could imagine their disgust at being sent out on such a night to call on so mean a cottage. I said I hoped they had treated her politely.

"Of course," she said, surprised, as she took off her cloak. "Fortunately I had some coins in my reticule and was able to reward them just now. Though"—her forehead wrinkled as she worried about the amount she had given them—"perhaps it was not wise. However," she went on, determined to deliver herself of her news, "there are great doings up at the house. My cousin, who is unwell, poor love, has received a visit from her husband's kinsman, Sir William Wynne, newly returned from putting down the rebellion in Ireland, who is of course accompanied by his servants and also a Captain he has attached to himself. A strange man . . ." Her voice tailed off as she went to the hallway to hang her cloak. "A *very* strange man!" she said as she returned, looking handsome. I noticed she had put on her blue stitched gown and her embroidered slippers for her visit to the manor. "Oh, there are plans for much entertainment! Mrs. Edward wishes me to help her with the arrangements, so tomorrow I am to spend all day with her there and you are to have a holiday, as Mr. Turner is to help with the conversation among the gentlemen."

I did not say to her what I thought: which was that if Sir William Wynne enjoyed flattery he would be well entertained by Mr. Turner. When Mr. Edward paid a visit to our schoolroom, which was not often, Mr. Turner bowed so low and so often that his nose turned white as his face reddened with his exertions. My mother must have seen something in my face, for she laughed and said, "There is no doubt Mr. Turner enjoys grand company. We must not forget he is a dependent whose livelihood depends on pleasing his employer. Besides, I sometimes enjoy it myself."

She said it so simply, and with such kindness towards Mr. Turner, also with so little sense of her own dependence other than one of gratitude, that I could not resist hugging her. Also, I have to confess, I hugged her with relief because it appeared that things were falling out well. I should be alone all the next day, my mother at the manor, and there would be time to think what should be done about the fugitive in the hut.

My mother disengaged herself from me, laughing, and saying that we must be getting to bed for the wicks of the lamps needed trimming—we lived by the daylight as much as we could in order to save the lamps. But she was still filled with gossip and as she put out the lamps and prepared our candles she told me that Sir William was a fine gentleman who wore highly colored clothes which she supposed must be the fashion. He was the Colonel of a volunteer regiment in nearby Wales called The

Ancient Britons; he paid the men out of his own pocket, and at the manor there had been much talk of politics and war: of the rising in Ireland and of the danger of invasion by our enemies the French. Sir William was in the neighborhood to recruit more volunteers and so was Captain Hunter Gowan, an Irish Protestant who had distinguished himself quelling the rebellion in another part of Ireland and who had become Sir William's henchman. "A dislikeable man, the Captain, Francis. Not a gentleman. Great pistols in his belt even in the library. He never sits, is never still, staring in people's faces as though he longs for an excuse to blow their brains out." She giggled at the thought of him. "He was like a rough soldier in a play, except that I think he would really shoot you, and not care. I suppose we need such men to defend us but he is unlike the officers I knew, friends of your father." She went to gather up my clothes which were again over the rail by the fire, but I prevented her and gathered them myself because there was still the mud upon them.

I lay in my bed very tired, half-dreaming, I suppose, and thought of colonels and recruiting captains, of rebellions and invasions and volunteer regiments of militia, all of which seemed somehow connected with the fate of the man in the hut. Then I saw the contorted face of a hanged man, his tongue stuck horribly from his mouth, a sight much worse than the one I had in fact seen, and somehow this dreadful face turned into a broad smile and the man sat up; it was my friend and he clapped me on the back and said, "Come *on!*"

When I opened my eyes at dawn I was wide-awake at once and full of anticipation as though it was Christmas morning. At first I could not remember why and then I remembered the fugitive and the way he depended on me.

My mother soon bustled off in great excitement, for she loved her cousin and our life in the cottage was very quiet. She went on foot this time, in pattens, for it was still very wet underfoot. As soon as I was alone I carefully cut some bacon, so that too great a helping would not be noticed, and put it in my pocket with two eggs and some bread. I also took a pan and this worried me more, for my mother might expect food to be gone but the disappearance of her pan would puzzle her. However, I resolved to have it back in its place before she returned. Then, putting some lumps of sea coal in my other pocket, for the stove in the hut, I set off up the bank.

By the time I was halfway up doubts began to crowd in my head. Suppose he was too ill for my help? I should have to tell my mother and then I could not guess what would happen to my friend, for she would have to tell others, and clearly there was some crime he had committed or at least some men who hated him. Suppose he had been discovered already or—he had seemed very ill—was dead?

As soon as I reached the lane at the top of the bank all these thoughts were driven from my mind. I darted back at once into the shelter of the trees, my heart beating, for in the field below, standing under the oak from which my friend had been hanged, was the figure of a man.

He was not one of the four I had seen last night but I guessed who he was at once, from my mother's description. Even at that distance I could see the pistols at his belt and sense a strange, pacing restlessness in his small body as he peered up and down and jerked his head this way and that, like a hen. He stooped quickly and picked something from the ground which he turned over in his hand, examining it closely. Then, if my heart had thumped before, it now began to beat so loud I thought the man below must hear it, *for he began to enter the copse.*

The hut in there was well hidden to a casual passer but nothing, I felt, could escape the intense, jerking attention of that distant head. I was about to cry out, to distract him, though what I should have done then I had no idea and to tell the truth there was something about that figure that made my blood cold, when there was a cry from another direction, from the copse itself; and a brown-clad man, bent low, broke from the trees and began to run in a direction that lay away from the hut. It was Caleb drawing him off, and I blessed his vigilance.

Captain Hunter Gowan, for I was sure it was he, called out, "Stop! Or I shoot!" and leveled one of his pistols. This astonished me, for although I knew nothing of the law, surely it was not possible in England to shoot a man running from a copse? Certainly it was not the Captain's land. Caleb must have reckoned likewise, for he continued running though taking the precaution to swerve a little, like a huge hare. This was just as well, for the Captain, shouting as though he had lost all control of himself, did indeed fire. Caleb stopped, slowly straightened himself, and turned to face his pursuer who advanced upon him waving his pistol like a madman. Soon they were face to face and I did not envy the Captain his first encounter with those cold blue eyes. I could not hear what was said, though the Captain was still shouting, and I saw Caleb lead off with the Captain behind him, pistol still in hand, as though he had put Caleb under arrest.

To see that man at the site of the hanging and see him

move towards the hut, to see Caleb appear and be led away and with him my only chance of help, left me stunned and frightened.

I forced myself to continue down the slope and towards the hut, wondering now how many pairs of eyes were on me as I crossed the open field.

But no one called after me and, taking a circular route through the copse, looking about me carefully before I lifted the brambles that more or less concealed the little door, I knocked on it three times, hoping the knock sounded more like that of a friend than the hammering of an enemy. There was no answer from inside.

After waiting, I fearfully lifted up the latch, pushed open the door against some obstruction on the floor, and saw that all was dark inside except for a tiny glow at the bottom of the stove. Then I stepped in, over what I saw now were clothes crammed to seal off the door, and found myself enveloped in a fug so hot and thick it was like a furnace, but one with a distinct reek of brandy on its breath. I shut the door and leaned towards the bunk, feeling over it with my hands. It was empty. Then fingers fastened very hard round my ankles and a hard voice said quietly, "Friend or foe—as if it mattered!"

"Friend, sir," I said and there was a small laugh from under the bed.

"I could wish you found me in nobler circumstances, boy. Here, move aside while I get the blazes out of this and find a light. Is that fellow still outside?"

"No, Caleb has drawn him off."

"Your ruffian friend? I fear I have brought troubles on you all. Ah well." He added the last with no note of apology in his voice. Soon he had pulled himself out from under the bunk and had a stub of candle burning. He sat on the bunk and by the light of the candle I saw his drawn face smiling, a little abashed, as though embarrassed to have been found under the bed. He was still draped in sackcloth but he had on his boots and a kerchief round his neck right up to his chin to ease, or hide, the mark of the hanging. I was already gasping in the great heat of the hut, but I saw the cleverness of it. Either he or Caleb had turned the hut into a sweat house, the heavy clothes blocking the window and the crack under the door blocked too. In this way he could sweat out his fever and, though his face was thin and white, he appeared to have done so.

"We cling to our lives absurdly," he said, pulling his sackcloth robe about him. "When I heard the crackle of that feller's feet I was under the bed before I knew it. Yet if he found me there I'd be helpless laughing."

He seemed strong; he was almost laughing now at himself.

"I've brought you some food and some coals for the fire."

"You are good, but not coals—they smoke."

He must have seen I was ashamed not to have thought of that because he added quickly, "It was a good thought, though. Your friend—Caleb is it?—left me a stock of dry stuff last night, though where he found it in that wet, God knows. A man of means! But food, did you say? I could eat this hut!" And taking the pan from me he put it on the stove, put the bacon into it, the eggs and the bread, and almost at once, so hot was the stove, the hut was filled with the familiar, comforting smell. When it was ready he seemed to devour it at a mouthful, took a draught from the flask I had seen Caleb offer him the night before, and sat down heavily on the bed, saying as though to himself,

"We may get out of this one yet." Then he said to me, "Who is this Caleb?"

I told him he was a famous poacher, never caught except for fighting, and he laughed. Then he asked about the pistol shot and I told him of that, and of the way the man who fired the shot had appeared to arrest Caleb to take him before the magistrate. He nodded and whistled. "Hunched man in a yellow coat who looks as though he'll hang himself if he can't find anyone else to hang? I knew the voice. Something must have disappointed him. Now, I wonder *what?*" and he grinned at me. "What's your name?" I told him I was called Francis. "A shepherd boy, did you say?" He looked at me carefully, sidelong, and I wondered if I had been remembering my Gloucestershire voice. It seemed to matter less, now that I knew him. "Are you indeed. My name's Jack. Sometime captain in His Majesty's Army, sometime other things, presently—in trouble." He seemed inclined to make a joke of his situation, but he must have known it was desperate if he was not inside the law. I tried to find out whether he was or not.

"Sir, shall I tell the magistrate about the men last night who tried to hang you?"

"Yes, if you want to see me hanged again. Do you?"

I did not answer that, instead I asked boldly, "Where do you come from?"

"From Ireland, the holy land of Ireland, as my friends do, the ones we met last night, and you saw how holy we were . . . I need another day and a night here. Can it be done?"

I was doubtful. "I'll help you," I said, "as much as I can. But Caleb can help you more."

"Will the magistrate keep him, d'you think?"

I did not think so. Mr. Edward was the magistrate and dearly though he would have loved to stop Caleb's poachings, he was always very careful with him because no one could ever be found who would give evidence against Caleb. Besides, I guessed he would be greatly angered at Captain Hunter Gowan for shooting at a man on his land. I told the Captain this.

"Well, we shall have to hope. I need friends. And, look, I need money. This. Can you sell it for me? Don't take a penny less than a hundred and fifty guineas, stick at that, you'll get it. It's worth twice."

He had taken the jeweled crucifix from his neck and was offering it to me. I began to stammer, because of his trust, because I had no idea how to sell such a thing, and because I could not understand why the ruffians had not taken it. At last I managed to say, "But why did those men—"

"Not steal it? Because they're Catholics. They nearly did, though." He smiled.

The word "Catholics" interested me because I had heard much about Irish Catholics, how they were poor and barbarous and lay in wait for landlords and cut them to pieces. But my mother had told me not to credit all such stories, although many Irish were indeed poor, and she had told me that Englishmen had all been Catholics once, which I knew to be true. So I said, "Do all Catholics behave like that?"

"Leave men to die with money round their necks?"

"Yes, and hang men?"

He raised his brows and pretended to be shocked. "So you think a Protestant would have had the cross quick enough? But how do you know I'm not a Catholic myself?"

"Because they tried to hang you!"

"A Catholic not hang a Catholic?" He made a noise like a laugh but it clearly hurt his throat. "You don't think it's just the English put down the Irish, do you? The Irish themselves do it well enough—though the English do better!"

"But my mother says the rebellion is the poor Catholics against their Protestant landlords."

"Does she now?" He looked at me, surprised. "Your mother sounds a fine woman. Well—there's Catholic landlords, some—and there's Catholics who don't want to lose their positions and there's poor Catholic Cork men who think poor Catholic Wexford men are the sons of the devil himself, and there's others who think the land will become Godless altogether if the rebels succeed. And"— he said it almost as though the thought amused him— "there's some who like the money and the slaughter. There's always those. But your mother's right, the fight's about property, *that*'s what excites men, especially if they have it. The Protestants have the property and they're scared to madness the Catholics'll have it off them. Poor, desperate dogs who can't own a horse or a gun. The Protestants have plenty of both and form yeomanry regiments who knock the daylights out of men armed with pitchforks . . . You like the sound of that?" He cocked his head on one side and stared at me. "You're a damned genteel shepherd boy!" I said nothing, and after a pause during which he continued to examine me, he went on, "Talking of property. Will you sell the cross? If I asked Caleb, they'd have him in jail on suspicion. But it's not stolen. That could be important when you come to sell it. I'll love you forever. I do already. Now go, will you? Do it. You can. I've work to do. I'm stiff as a plank and I've to

loosen myself before I step out of this hut." He suddenly
sounded tired, though he still smiled at me. "Wait. Are
we not near a place called Cheltenham, where there's
gaming?"

I told him that fashionable people from London went
there to take the waters and I believed there were games
of cards in the new Assembly Rooms though I had never
been to them.

He was delighted to hear this and said where there was
gaming there were losses and people would need to raise
money quickly, so there would be places where things
like the cross could be sold without too many questions
being asked.

But there was one more question I had to ask him.
Even though he was weak he seemed filled with energy
and quickness whereas the men who had dragged him to
this spot had been dull and heavy, not even good hang-
men as it turned out. So I gathered my courage and said,
"How did those men catch you?"

He looked at me for a moment. "If you'd asked where,
or why, that's a long story. But *how*—ah!" and he tapped
the brandy flask. "Too much of this. Not often, but sometimes. They'd never have got me else! I knew they were
on the boat with me—good God, how could I mistake
them!—so I played a little game when we landed. If
we drank together I had them under my eye. Well," he
shrugged, "I played too high." Then he burst out, "They
were a kind of soldier, boy, can you believe it? With the
King's money in their pockets for murdering their own
kind. God help the King if he saw some of his friends.
The King's Army rubs its eyes when it sees them! . . .
But—money. I need a suit of clothes, a good horse and
pistols. I need to get out of here. Will you do it for me?

Will you?" He put his head on one side again, in the way
he had, so sure of my help, so forgetful of his absurd and
vulnerable appearance, white-faced in his robe of sacking,
that I felt he put himself into my power. Though I had no
idea how to do what he asked, I promised myself that I
would not disappont him. He seemed so confidently to expect that I would find a way.

4

The Jeweled Cross

So I left him, and crossed the field, wondering what became of Caleb but quite sure he would give a good account of himself. The cross was round my neck and under my shirt, seeming almost to burn a hole in my chest because of my consciousness of its importance and value.

It was still early; the sky was gray and I could not see the sun, but I knew it had not risen high by the feel of the air. This was good because it became clear to me, as I thought about it, that if I was to get into Cheltenham and back, having sold the cross, without anyone knowing, it would have to be today while my mother was occupied at the manor.

Cheltenham was a town barely known to us, though only lying some eight miles distant, at the foot of the hills. Our town was Gloucester, about the same distance away though in another direction, because to our way of thinking Cheltenham was a newfangled place, given over to pleasure and to strangers. It had used to be a little market town, but when I was a baby, newly arrived in these parts from Yorkshire, His Majesty the King came there to drink the healing waters, and after that the fashionable world came there also, to drink at the Royal Well. Fine houses were built, and theaters, and an assembly room for dancing and card games. I had only been there once, and though there were some fine buildings, I thought it a messy sort of place, all one long street and a bog across which they were beginning to lay a road. However, such is the power of fashion, my mother told me, that however beautiful and ancient our beloved town of Gloucester, with its great cathedral, if Cheltenham was the place where people of fashion had decided to gather, Cheltenham it must be.

My only hope of getting there this day lay with Joel the carrier. He made his way to our village about midmorning, delivering and collecting parcels and packages, returning to Gloucester by way of every inn that lay on his road down into the plain. He delivered more packages at these inns and collected others, but he also took on a certain amount of freight himself, of a liquid kind; and Joel asleep at his reins, with his patient horse leading them both to Gloucester, was one of the sights of our county.

However, if he would give me a ride, I should not have to wait outside too many inns, because I would ask him to put me down at the turn-off to Gloucester, and make the rest of the journey to Cheltenham on foot.

I sat on the wall of Manor Farm awaiting him. Some village lads were there: Tom Holder, Hiram Savory, and Caleb's son, Daniel. It was a great meeting place for us, and pennies were to be earned by doing odd jobs. I was not allowed to do these jobs by Mr. Edward, who said it was unfitting, but I did them sometimes nevertheless. We boys were friendly enough, although they were all a little on their guard against me because of my connection with the manor, but there was nothing I could do about that. Tom Holder had heard about the carriage last night, and said a foreign general had come to visit the manor; Hiram said it was Bonaparte himself, come to sue for peace. No one, I was relieved to hear, knew anything of the events last night at the oak tree. I suppose a stranger, seeing us there talking, kicking our legs on the wall, would have thought us stupid and dull, talking nonsense, but it was not really like that, not when you knew. It was a sort of game. The visitors at the manor were of no interest to anyone but me, and all that happened at the big house, though significant to their lives, was to them as indifferent and unpredictable as the weather. In fact they despised their masters, or rather they despised the control their masters had over them, in a way that would have surprised Mr. Edward. They were so quick and lively and free with each other, as no one was in Mr. Edward's house—except Mrs. Edward, who tried to be but sometimes looked rather damped—and to the manor these boys and their fathers were only dun-colored figures to be passed in a carriage, or summoned to perform some task.

Joel at last came, making his slow way up the lane, and it was difficult for me to talk to him alone, because I did not want the others to know where I was going. I managed it by beckoning him to one side, and when I did that he touched his hat respectfully, thinking I had some commission for him from the manor. My friends saw this, and it was another black mark against me I am sure, but I could see no other way of talking to him privately.

After keeping me in suspense, as I knew he would, he agreed to take me with him part of the descent until he turned off on one of his errands. He was glad of the company, I dare say, for Joel was a sociable man. But of course he must first have his yarn within-doors and his cup of cider. At last he came out of the dairy and exchanged some lengthy chaff with the boys. For Joel, the longer he took over anything the better, and besides I had betrayed impatience, which with Joel was a very great mistake. I saw him looking at me with amusement as I chafed and he lingered.

In the end, however, he climbed slowly up into his seat, taking the reins in his great hands and, at last, I wedged myself among his bales and packages behind him. Each of these was wrapped in stout sackcloth stitched together, or secured with twine, as though bound on journeys to China or the Indies, though they would each be taken only a few miles. Daniel ran behind the cart for a while, teasing me, and he did not have to run very fast to keep up. I whispered to him to be off, I did not want my mother to know I was taking this journey, and this he understood and stopped, turning and making his way back to the yard.

As soon as he was gone, I put my head down in the back of Joel's cart. As we passed the last cottage I sat up, reasonably satisfied that no one had seen me on my journey, and soon we were at the top of the steep hill called Bubb's that was the beginning of the long descent down into the plain. Here Joel made me dismount with him, to lessen the weight, and told me to pull back at the tail-board to prevent the cart slipping. So we continued, the wheels locked in an iron shoe, I pulling the cart, he hold-ing back the head of his patient horse whose shoes slipped so often on the gradient that we seemed in danger of landing in a pile at the bottom, one on top of the other. However, Joel and his horse managed it, as they always did, and soon we were on a gentler slope. Now I mounted beside him, for the road was lonely, there was little chance of being seen, and I had decided to see if Joel could help me with my quest. Besides, it was very cold in the back, it was a gray east-windy sort of a day, and the prospect of pressing against the huge side of Joel, as any passenger had to in order not to fall off, was inviting.

The problem about gaining his help was that I could tell him no more of the difficulty than was necessary. Joel was a great repository of gossip, indeed he paid for his flagons of ale in that way, and he was known to be better and quicker than a newspaper.

So I began by asking him if he knew where I could dispose of a small valuable.

"A boy's valuable would it be, or a grown-up valuable?" he asked judiciously, the reins slack in his hand as we slowly continued.

"A grown-up one," I answered, and he turned his head to look at me.

"A valuable valuable, as it might be."

"A valuable." This was taking us in circles. "The truth is, Joel, I have a friend who is in some small money trou-ble, and he wishes me to sell something belonging to him. It is a matter of some delicacy." This last was a phrase I had heard used.

"Ah! Delicate, eh? I wouldn't have much to do with

delicate things like that. Not me. You, now, that's different."

Teasing is a popular sport among our country people, they hate to do anything straightforwardly. It is second nature to them, but it is not part of my nature and now I found myself not far from tears.

"A watch perhaps is it? Gold, I dare say?"

"If you cannot help me I must take my chance," I said, utterly miserable.

"A jewel maybe?" He paused. "Cannot help you? Wouldn't say *cannot*."

"Will not, then."

"Depends." He seemed to be thinking. "There is a place . . . No, that wouldn't do, I dare say. Don't have much cause to sell *valuables* myself. Not being so *delicate*. A jewel, you said."

"A . . . trinket."

"Ah." He looked at me with interest for the first time. "I *see*. Why didn't you say so afore? I've always had a great respect for your mother. Why didn't you say so first off? Just by the Tap Room there. Small secret sort of a place. Buys secret too, I dare say. Mind you get the price though. Know the price? Got to know the price whether you sell *or* buy."

"I think so," I said, the thought of my secret, and the vast sum involved, making me more and more nervous.

When we came to the bend in the road that would take Joel over the hill and down into Gloucester, on his round-about route from farm to farm, he stopped the cart and I thanked him and began to climb down. He allowed me to get my foot on the iron rung that stuck out from the side of the cart, before he said, "And where are you going?"

I turned awkwardly to look up at him, half-on and

half-off his cart, and said irritably enough, "Why, Cheltenham, of course!" and he laughed and went into a rig-
marole about if I preferred to walk the last four miles that
was all the same to him, but the upshot of it was, and he
took an age before he put me out of my impatience and
irritation, that he had a commission to do in Cheltenham
anyway, and if I wished—only if I *wished* of course—I
could ride with him all the way to the town.

This was a stroke of good fortune for me, because I had
to get through my business and be home before nightfall.
But I was more cross than content when I settled myself
once more into the seat beside him. There seemed no end
to his fooling with me. My sulks put Joel into a huge good
humor. He chuckled most of the way from that moment
on, the shoulders of his coat heaving up and down.
"'Why, Cheltenham of *course*,' he says, and I say, 'Well,
that's funny because I be going there myself,'" and so on
and on, causing himself great amusement.

The road was very bad and steep and, after the rain,
was the course of many young rivers. Soon, on our left
shoulder, a huge gorse-covered hill loomed so close it
seemed about to topple over us. Joel saw me looking up at
it and he said, "We bless that hill, we carriers. 'Tis called
Windsarse Hill," and he cackled and heaved some more.
The empty downs rolled and fell away to our right, but
the great height of that hill and its nearness to us made
that part of the journey seem dark and awesome. The
pale sun behind us was like a mildewed lemon, because it
was draped in as many layers of quickly blown gray
clouds as Joel was draped in overcoats. Then the way
grew steep again, even steeper than before, and we dismounted onto the hopelessly ruined road, and soon my
boots and stockings and breeches were in as bad a case as

they had been in the night before. But Joel and his horse managed it to the bottom, and I began to have a respect for both of them and for the hardness of their lives.

At Southfield Farm, its gray chimneys smoking—and I was glad to find Joel had no business there—we were at last on the plain, and not long after, we were at the turnpike house at the entrance to the town. It was a clean white building, hung with lamps, and here Joel paid his due. I learned from him that it was called Gallows Oak Pike, a place where they used to hang highwaymen and thieves, and the aptness of the name made my stomach lurch.

But I was cheered by the appearance of the town. The long High Street still had some of the old thatched houses, but among them had been built high thin ones of smooth stone, and they gave an air of elegance to the place, set back from well-laid pavements broader than any I had seen. It was easy to imagine them paced by well-dressed ladies and gentlemen in the months of summer, and although there were few of these at this season, there were enough, and enough fine carriages, to give the place an air of excitement.

At a building marked in great painted letters PLOUGH INN & COFFEE ROOMS, Joel halted the cart, telling me he had his business inside there and this was the end of our journey. I had known he would not make the ascent of those two terrible hills again this day, indeed I wondered how his horse managed to climb them at all, but I felt very alone and woeful, standing there in my mud-bespattered clothes and was loath to part with him.

He pointed to a fine building and told me it was the Assembly Room, and up the side of it I would find a jeweler's for my "valuable"—upon which there was more heaving of the great shoulders, but we parted friendly enough, as, telling me earnestly to make sure that I got the best price, he turned cheerfully into the yard of the inn. And he had indeed cheered me. Things did not seem quite so difficult and fearful after being with Joel.

I found the jeweler's shop easily, because although it was tucked up a narrow alley, there were all sorts of rich things in its two bow-fronted windows: silver candlesticks and chafing dishes, rings and necklaces displayed on stands of purple velvet, repeater watches, pairs of pistols embossed with silver wire in beautiful designs, and behind them all was a notice which read: *Articles of Value Exchanged at the Most Favorable Rates.*

Through the panes in the top half of the little black door that stood between the two curved windows, I could see more rich objects inside, winking and shining in the meager light that reached them from the street. So, feeling the cross under my shirt with my fingers like a talisman, I pressed the latch of the door and pushed it open to the jangling of a bell; and closing it carefully behind me, to further janglings of the bell, I found myself, heart beating, standing in the murky light of a small shop that looked to me as stuffed with priceless treasure, as magical and astonishing as the cave of Aladdin itself.

5

Mr. Edward

Behind the counter there were two little steps that led to
another door. This also had windows in it and as I grew
accustomed to the half-light I became aware that I was
being watched through it. The owner of the face that I
could dimly see took his time about coming into the shop
to ask what I wanted so I guessed I was being examined.
It was clear that I was not found to be interesting, for
when the door did open a pale young man appeared who
leaned on the side of it not looking at me and said,
"Well?" as he explored the inside of his mouth with his
little finger.

"I have something to sell and I would be pleased if you
would buy it," I said.

He now came down the stairs and looked at me. But he
soon found it more interesting to examine the tip of his
finger which he had withdrawn from his mouth and now
wiped in his armpit. "Show," he said, yawning.

I had reason to be grateful to him. I think any sort of
behavior would have discomfited me more. But this sort,
from certain kinds of older people, any boy is accustomed
to and learns to let it wash over him. I did not mind this
young man one jot.

So I reached inside my shirt, hooked the string over my
head and advanced the cross towards him in my fist,
opening my hand to reveal it when it was under his nose,
feeling warmed by my sight of its richness.

The young man picked it from my palm with two
fingers, held it up and said, "Paste. We might manage
half a sovereign." Then he dropped the cross on a piece of
green baize that protected the glass top of the counter
and leaned towards me, his face unpleasantly close to
mine.

I was bitterly disappointed. I know nothing about
jewels, and although the rich winking of the little brilliants that were set into the cross made it hard for me to
believe they were worthless, there was still the mystery of
why those men had not bothered to steal it. Perhaps they
had known. Perhaps Captain Jack was deceived about its
value.

I could not sell it for that. As I reached for the cross so
did the young man, saying, "There may be a penny or
two more of value in it. Wait here," and retreated back up
the two steps into the inner room not much more quickly
than he had descended them, but a little. I began once
more to hope.

After a few moments an older man, whom I took to be

the Mr. Donaldson whose name I had seen above the door of the shop, if anything taller and thinner than his assistant, came out of the back room and down the steps, the cross in his hand, the young man glaring at me from behind his shoulder.

The older one looked at me for a short space over his little glasses; then, putting back his head and raising his brows, he looked down carefully through them at the cross which he had laid in his palm. Then up at me again and down at the cross until I began to feel very uncomfortable and tried to compose my face in order to conceal my anxiety.

"May I inquire where you got this?" he said at last in a quiet voice.

"That I am not at liberty to tell you, sir. The party who entrusted it to me did not wish his identity to be known. He does, however, know the figure for which he is willing to part with it."

After this speech Mr. Donaldson examined me again, without speaking. "Indeed. And what would that figure be?"

"A hundred and fifty guineas, sir," I said, and the young man snorted. Mr. Donaldson showed no reaction when I mentioned the price but continued to examine the cross.

"I see," he said. "Of course there is always the possibility that this piece, if it is of that value and I do not say that it is, may have been stolen."

"I swear, sir—"

"I do not say that you have stolen it nor would you admit it if you had. No, it is the history of the piece that is missing." He looked at me again. "If your friend— through no fault of his own—should find himself *not* the rightful owner, we should have to return it to whomever *was* that owner with consequent loss to ourselves. That is, if we had bought it. You can tell me no more? I see. It will be necessary for us to have your name and address."

This I gave him, on a piece of paper he offered, putting my name and feeling uncomfortable at how near this was coming to my mother. Mr. Donaldson kept his eyes on me all the time I was writing and I found myself trying so hard to give an honest appearance that I began to feel as if I had indeed stolen it. I also had a feeling, however, that Mr. Donaldson was accustomed to keeping confidences and my silence was not entirely mysterious to him. I noticed he did not let his assistant see my name and address but folded the paper four times and put it into his watch pocket.

"Good. That is settled then. And the price is a fair one."

"You mean you will buy it? May I have the money?" I was so overjoyed that it came out like a shout.

"Not quite so quick as that. Both parties must be satisfied. *You* are satisfied. And eager to be off. Why so eager? That is a question I am bound to ask myself. What do you say to that?" He was smiling at me but watching me. Of course I knew he was playing with me a little, as the snigger of the young man testified.

"I have given you my name, and the cross. What more do you want of me?" I said, trying to keep tears out of my voice because of course it was anger, not tears, that made my voice sound odd. It had been the same with Joel.

"Is it your *true* name? If we came in search of you, should we find such a name and such a residence and you there to answer? You see? Is there, for example, anyone in the town who could vouch for you?"

There was only Joel, if I could find him, and I had the feeling that he would make such a mystery of vouching for me, and enjoy himself so much, he would leave me under deeper suspicion than before. There seemed no end to my difficulties.

While I stood there, at a loss, the two men looking at me, the bell above the door of the shop gave such an angry jangle it was clear that someone had entered with more firmness and resolve than I had been able to show. The eyes of both men shifted past me to the door and their expressions changed: Mr. Donaldson's to one of grave courtesy and the thin young man's to a sort of cringing leer.

"Ah, Mr. Edward, sir. Your job is quite done. Go fetch Mrs. Edward's necklace, will you?" Mr. Donaldson said to his assistant who promptly made to depart saying as he did so, "Watch him!" because in my great fright at seeing my guardian enter the shop I had shrunk as far as I could to the darkest corner. Mr. Edward turned, saw me, and said with his usual coolness, for he made it a point of honor never to appear surprised, "Sir? Why do I find you here?"

Before I had need to answer, the assistant returned with a long black jewel box and, hearing Mr. Edward address me, said, with great astonishment, "You know him, sir?"

The way in which Mr. Edward turned to answer the assistant's question showed me that nothing more fortunate could have happened. Mr. Edward clearly regarded his intervention as the height of impertinence and Mr. Donaldson began to tap his fingers impatiently, fixing a warning glance on his assistant that the young man was too startled by Mr. Edward's expression to take account of.

"I do," said Mr. Edward.

"In what capacity?" said the young man, determined to brazen it out and emboldened, I felt sure, by irritation at me. He disliked being found in the capacity of a shop assistant by someone younger and, as I became more and more miserably aware in the exquisitely dressed presence of Mr. Edward, so much dirtier than himself.

"He is a member of my household, sir," said Mr. Edward, but the assistant still persevered despite the looks and hums and tappings of his master. "Honest is he? I mean . . . it is important . . . but of course if you . . ." His voice died away entirely as Mr. Edward's head went back so far that his eyes narrowed almost to disappearance and the young man looked like being turned to ashes by flame blasts from Mr. Edward's carefully aimed nostrils.

"That will do," said his master. "Make out the note of hand for the sum agreed. And look sharp!" The young man almost fell up the steps in his eagerness to be gone. Smiling and murmuring, Mr. Donaldson had opened the black box and was making much fuss over its contents, a fine necklace of yellow stones, telling Mr. Edward what a joy it was to clean such a beautiful piece and how he had spent much of the day before repairing one of the links so that Mrs. Edward might have it for this night. Mr. Edward said nothing, merely picked up the box and put it in the inside pocket of his coat, stiffening when the assistant entered—he almost sidled in this time—with a paper that he handed to Mr. Donaldson. The jeweler looked it over, excusing himself to Mr. Edward, signed it, folded it and handed it to me politely saying, "There, I think you will find that is in order," and immediately began to bow us both out of his shop.

I had sold the cross! But Mr. Edward would surely now
begin to question me. On the pavement outside the shop
he looked at me, little spots of color in his cheeks, but I
could see he was still trying to recover from the insult he
considered himself to have received: someone had ques-
tioned him about the honesty of a dependent. His eyes
were on my face but distant, as though he did not see me
at all, and then they shifted to the roadway behind me. A
carriage was approaching us, with armorial blazons on its
door, and as it passed a wave from inside it made Mr. Edward raise his hat carefully a few inches and bow, almost
unnoticeably, but with something that was very nearly
a smile on his face.

"My lord Fauconberg," he said, half to me and half to
the road. Then he recollected himself and with a specu-
lating glance after the carriage, as though he would like
in a moment to exchange a few words with its occupant,
he turned, rather reluctantly, to me. "You are not very—
neat, Francis. How did you get here?" I told him. "How
shall you return?" I told him I should walk.

"You shall not," he said, without kindness, or at least
with none that I could detect, though I sometimes wondered with Mr. Edward. He was a stiff man but I never
received an *un*kindness from him. "Have you eaten?" he
asked me. I told him not and began to say that this did
not matter, though as soon as he put the idea in my head
I realized I was horribly hungry. He cut me short, bowing
to some passing acquaintances. He was clearly in a social
mood which made my presence an irritation to him. He
raised his cane to another gentleman who was approaching, then he drew a purse from his pocket and gave me a
shilling. "There is a good Ordinary at the Bell Inn over
there—do you see it? Do not stop long and avoid the com-

pany. Now, off with you. Stay—how shall you return? Ask the landlord there to give you a horse in my name—I say, ostler!" He called to a whistling young man in boots who was leading a horse by the bridle in the direction of the Bell. "You know me, do you not?" "I do, sir," said the other cheerfully. "Be good enough to present my compliments to your master and say I will be grateful to him if he will see this young man mounted for the journey to Elstone. I shall return the horse myself within two days." "Very good, sir," said the ostler beginning again on his way to the Bell and recommencing his whistling. "Go with him," said Mr. Edward, "and Francis—endeavor to make your appearance less of a . . . less . . ."—he waved his hand at my clothes, frowning—"when next you come to town. Ah, Sir Joshua, how do you? Shall we be seeing you this afternoon?" and more such pleasantries to a stout gentleman who had come up. Altogether he showed a more genial Mr. Edward than I had guessed existed, as I made good my escape. Before I was quite away I saw my old adversary of the jeweler's shop looking at me through the door and he stuck out his tongue at me. Feeling more lively than I had done at any time that day I took pleasure in doing the same to him.

Soon, well pleased with myself, I was ensconced in the snug at the Bell with a hot pie, a mug of beer and leisure to examine my achievement thus far.

A ride all the way into town and a horse to take me back again and the jeweled cross sold. Then I remembered the paper Mr. Donaldson had given me and I took it out, first making sure I was alone. It was a note, signed by him, promising to pay whoever carried it to him the sum we had agreed upon. I was relieved not to have that number of guineas in my pocket, for I had heard of foot-

pads on the road beyond the turnpike. I put the paper
back inside my shirt so that it nestled there behind the
waistband of my breeches, held in place by my belt,
which I tightened. Anyone who found that would have to
kill me first, I told myself bravely, greatly heartened by
the pie and the beer and, I dare say, thinking myself a
fine fellow. But at once my heart, which I had thought to
be so stout, turn to jelly again. Because at that moment I
heard, behind the thin partition wall that separated my
snuggery from the taproom, the last voices in the world
that I wanted to hear: the voices, that I now knew to be
Irish, of the rogues I had met the previous night.

They had just come in. I could hear the scraping of
chairs and the call for brandy, and through a crack in the
paneling I saw three of the men I had seen at the hanging. The long-haired one I had taken to be their leader
was not with them. There was a fourth man, however,
and him they appeared to be trying to make drunk, even
drunker than they were themselves. They lighted pipes of
tobacco and soon sprawled at their ease, and more than
once I saw one of their number tip part of his glass of
spirits into that of the fourth man when he seemed not to
be looking. From their conversation I understood what
they were about. They were trying to talk their companion into volunteering. I had heard of such recruiting.
These were "head" men, paid so much a head for every
wretch they could entrap into joining them, and of
course, once there, he could only escape at the risk of terrible punishment.

Their talk was of the wars in Ireland and they seemed
to have chosen their man well, for he laughed at their de-
scriptions. They told him he should have the delight of
preparing a pitch cap for a rebel, which they said was a

cap of tar put over a prisoner's head and set alight. They said gunpowder could be rubbed in first to make the blaze even more jolly. They all laughed at this and were such terrible men that whatever Captain Jack had done I did not care. If these were his enemies, then he was more than ever my friend.

I felt quite certain that these must be the Irish soldiers of Hunter Gowan and that they were now trying to swell the ranks of Sir William Wynne's regiment of Ancient Britons. This was mostly composed of Welshmen, my mother had told me, for Sir William raised the regiment in Wales, but I supposed he had lost men in Ireland and had come as far afield as our county in order to recruit more.

They painted the delights of their life in such colors that at last the drunk man narrowed his eyes and asked, shrewdly, if it was all such sport why were they not still at it, what were they doing here? They said they had business. Some damned rogue captain had begun directing the rebels—they did not know who he was; "Captain Moonlight" they called him—but with his help the rebels had become more dangerous. Up till then it had been as easy as shooting rabbits. "So you got rid of him, boys?" said the man. "That we did," they said. The one who had held the lamp at the hanging began to laugh. "John Quillen knew his face but the damned Captain didn't know John's. We followed him to Bristol, drank with him there, begod, nice and polite. John was behind the door. 'Twas easy!" "What would you know of it?" growled one of the other men. "You were twice as drunk as he was." "So the hell were you!" his companion replied angrily, and before a fight could break out the Gloucestershire man, eager I suppose to hear the rest of the story, broke in and said, "So you did for him there?" "Not at all," said the talkative one. "We had our orders." He mimed the wringing of a neck. "And it wasn't so far from where we sit now!" At this point one of the others told him to shut his mouth.

I crept away, wishing to be as far from them as I could. The ostler was as good as his word and soon, on a fine horse, the note of hand inside my clothes, I was returning the way I had come with Joel. For all his teasing, I missed Joel as the dusk came down; those men had been frightening and Joel seemed all that was friendly and familiar in my old world.

6

Captain Hunter Gowan

When I reached our village I judged it best to go straight to the manor, to deliver the horse there. When I reached the stables I found Mr. Edward had returned before me, but not by much, for his beautiful black horse, Nimrod, was being attended to by a groom and he still steamed a little in the cold evening air.

Going round to the front of the house I encountered Mr. Edward in the hall, frowning and flushed, with a man I recognized as the one who had shot at Caleb. He had red hair and a blotched complexion and I did not wonder that my mother had not liked him, for there was something wolfish about his visage; his pale eyes protruded, darting about in a dreadful impatience. He looked all the time as though he were about to burst, though at this moment he was trying to force a smile on his face in order to placate Mr. Edward who was clearly very angry. Indeed Mr. Edward seemed to have some difficulty in containing himself also, but he was striving to be courteous because, as I saw, this man was some kind of officer and a guest in his house.

Mr. Edward brushed aside my thanks for the horse and my account of where I had left it with a hasty "Yes, yes" and was clearly about to tell me to be gone when, as I supposed, he remembered the cause of our encounter in the town and said, "Your mother is busy preparing for the entertainment of our guests, but doubtless you have something to impart to her." So I understand that Mr. Edward, like Joel, had understood I was selling some piece of jewelry of my mother's, and he regarded the matter as beneath his dignity to inquire into. Or, again, maybe I was doing him a wrong. Perhaps he felt she was entitled to privacy in whatever small arrangements she made. Certainly I approved his evident dislike of the Captain. Then another thing happened to distract poor Mr. Edward who, what with his indignation at Captain Hunter Gowan and his anxiety about the near arrival of his guests, was more near to losing his perfect composure than I had ever seen him. This last distraction was the slow descent of the stairs of the fattest, most brilliant gentleman I had ever seen.

He was all color. From the top of his old-fashioned powdered wig to his huge red face, to his waistcoat stretched across his vast stomach shining like a peacock's tail, to his cutaway coat in sky-blue satin with gold lace at the edges and breeches and stockings of the same color, down to the huge buckles studded with brilliants in his red cloth shoes, he shone and glittered like a walking ballroom, or like a flagship illuminated for the triumph of an admiral.

"And who is this jackanapes?" he said as he came down the staircase, puffing slightly, and with some attempt at affability. Company was expected, after all, and he was clearly dressed for it. I doubted that even this extraordinary personage dressed in this way every night.

"This is my kinsman, Francis Place," said Mr. Edward, "somewhat the worse for wear I fear," he added with a glance at my clothes.

"F—rancis P—lace," said Captain Hunter Gowan, his eyes for once still, and fastened on my face. "He has doubtless been riding, from the state of his clothes. From whence, I wonder?"

"From town. We met there. Now really, Sir William, with your permission I must have some private words with your—adjutant. It is a matter that closely concerns my position in the county. You must forgive me."

"What?" wheezed the old gentleman. "Tom in a scrape? Best recruiting captain in the country. Best dam' soldier."

So this was Sir William Wynne. I had already guessed so from my mother's description. If he commanded one of the best regiments of irregulars that had been in Ireland, this did not recommend him to me, when I remembered what I had heard in the Bell. It was hard to think of this fat man commanding anything. Surely Captain Hunter Gowan did his work for him. It was he who now spoke.

"Mr. Edward, sir, of course, we shall talk together. It will give me all the pleasure in the world. But first—may I ask where your young kinsman lives? I have not seen him in your house before."

"In a cottage to the east of the village," said Mr. Edward shortly, his nostrils rising, as they had in the shop.

"That would be near the top road?"

"I dare say."

"Might I speak with him? After we have spoken together, of course."

"Why, sir?"

"There were doings, I believe, in that direction last night. These are troubled times, Mr. Edward, dangerous times, more so than perhaps you realize—being a country gentleman." Though he smiled, Captain Hunter Gowan managed to make these last words perfectly insulting. "Your—kinsman—may have heard, or seen, something to the purpose." Here he stared at me as though only hindered by the presence of the other two gentlemen from falling upon me and biting me.

"Did you, boy?"

"No, sir." Here, at least, my way was clear. If a lie would save Captain Jack, I was willing to blacken my soul.

"Nevertheless, Mr. Edward, if you would grant me perhaps five minutes with him—I have some small experience in these matters—" Here he bowed to Sir William Wynne who muttered, "Yes indeed. Ha!" and Captain Hunter Gowan went on, "He might have some small suggestion to make, some detail insignificant to him but not so to me, for he knows the place well."

"You make mysteries, sir," said Mr. Edward, who now gave up all attempt to disguise his dislike for the Captain. "But very well. Perhaps you would first come with me. Remain here, Francis."

Mr. Edward so seldom called me by name that despite my resistance to his coolness I felt pleased. He clearly ranged himself on my side against this dreadful Captain, and I was grateful for that.

I was left standing in the high hall with Sir William Wynne who seemed momentarily at a loss to be so deserted. He held a decorated snuffbox in one hand and set to tapping it with the other. "Don't hide anything from Captain Hunter Gowan, boy. King's business. Bound to be." He lost interest in me after that and began a progress to the far end of the hall where he came to a halt before the double doors of the drawing room. Here he waited until a footman appeared from nowhere to open them for him—and both had to be opened to allow the passing of that extraordinary figure—then closed them behind him with a flourish of the wrists and disappeared without looking at me.

This left me alone in the hall and I cautiously approached the door of the room inside which I could hear Mr. Edward's voice raised in anger.

"I don't care what you had 'reason to suspect,' sir! I know nothing of the events at which you hint so darkly and I care nothing, unless you choose to be open with me. If you are using this place for some scheme or for some damned politics, I will have none of it, do you hear? I have a position in this county. I am a magistrate and you may count yourself lucky that Bawcombe is content to agree that your pistol went off accidentally!"

Here the Captain murmured something in a surprisingly quiet style as though he was aware that he was in a delicate position. I could not hear what he said but it caused another explosion from Mr. Edward. "I'm perfectly aware he is a rascal, sir! I do not need you to tell me my business. I am astonished, however, that you think it a reason for shooting at him. This country is not at war,

sir. You are not in Ireland, sir. You are the companion of
my guest, Sir William Wynne, and that is the beginning
and end of our acquaintance. I shall require you while
you are under my roof to conduct yourself like a gentleman and remain within the strict limits of the law. Otherwise, as an upholder of the law, I shall be forced to detain
you, sir, with a greater show of justice than you used in
the detaining and questioning of Bawcombe."

"He knew more than he told me. I'm sure of it!"
Hunter Gowan's voice was raised now.

"Of what? And now there is to be further questioning
of the boy! I warn you."

Here there was more murmuring from Hunter Gowan
and a scraping of furniture and I had hardly time to seat
myself on a wooden settle on the opposite side of the hall
before the two men emerged.

When they did so it was clear that although Mr. Edward had a high color and Captain Hunter Gowan was as
blotched and yellow as ever, the two men had agreed to
keep up the appearance of some sort of accord in public.

The Captain's eye fell at once upon me and a light entered into it, as though I might be someone upon whom
he could vent his anger. "Ah, Master Francis Place . . .
Perhaps the five minutes you agreed to allow me?"

Mr. Edward hesitated but at that moment there was
the sound of a carriage coming up the drive and Mr. Edward, to whom too much was happening at once, said,
"Oh, very well, but for heavens' sake take him off to the
schoolroom, here are my guests!" Then the large bell on
the chain outside sounded and he withdrew to warn his
wife that guests were come.

So I found myself reluctantly leading the Captain up
the stairs, he bearing a lamp, to the gloomy room where I

and my cousins spent so many hours. He kept close behind me, as though to prevent me running away.

Once within the schoolroom he shut the door, motioned me to one of the desks and sat himself on the edge of Mr. Turner's.

"You were in Cheltenham today?"

"Yes."

"Why?"

I hesitated and in a rasping whisper, worse than a shout, he sped the word at me again, like a bullet. "*Why?*"

I had no time to invent; I had not been able to invent a reason all day, so I said, "I had a commission."

Captain Hunter Gowan went completely still and smiled down at the table. Then he looked up and said in a low voice, almost in a monotone, "Boy. When I ask a question I expect an answer to that question and not an answer that requires another question. Do—you—understand?" The last words he spoke in an even softer voice, with the smile still on his face, and nothing could have convinced me better that I was in the presence of a man who could kill me with pleasure. He now waited for my answer. I told him I was selling something for my mother. It was the best I could do.

He stared at me for what seemed a long while. Then he repeated my name, "Francis Place, Francis Place," and took something from his pocket which he put on the table beside him, looking down at it.

"Last night, did you hear horses and men?"

"No, sir."

"Nothing unusual?"

"No, sir."

"You were not out?"

"No, sir."

"What's this?" With a backhanded flick he threw my knife at me, the one with F.P. burned into the handle.

"My knife, sir. I must have dropped it."

"By the oak?"

"Possibly, sir."

"What oak?"

"The—big one near my house I supposed you to mean."

"When did you lose it? Some time ago?"

"Yes."

"There is no rust on it," he said with boredom, turning and looking out of the window, as though I was too unskillful a liar to retain his interest. Still looking out of the window he said, "I have had boys your age flogged till the flesh hung off their backs like rags for less than this. I cannot do that to you here, not now, but the time may come when you shall have cause to remember me. I give you one more chance." He turned to face me again. "This knife was found lying on disturbed ground, on hoofprints, and yet it had not been trodden on. Therefore it was dropped after the horses had gone. I found it at first light this morning. Therefore it fell during the night. *How did it get there?*" The veins on his neck stood out as he leaned forward.

"I don't know," I said. There was nothing else I could say.

"Show me the money you got in Cheltenham this morning."

"No, sir, it is a family matter."

"Family matter?" He screamed it. "You country squireens have an idea of your importance . . . And not a squireen either, a dependent, a pauper! Look at you! Show me the money!"

I sat still, frozen, and suddenly he jackknifed from the edge of the table and came for me. I jumped up and ran for the back of the room, pushing desks between myself and him. It crossed my mind that he was indeed going to kill me, even here in Mr. Edward's house, and justify himself afterwards.

But all along I had been relying on Mr. Edward's support and now I learned I had been right to do so. At the sound of shouting and of desks being moved there was the noise of the doorknob being turned and Mr. Edward stood in the doorway holding up a lamp. "Captain, the guests are assembled," he said, and Hunter Gowan bowed slightly, as though unable to trust himself to speak. Then Mr. Edward turned to me and said, with unusual kindness in his voice, "Francis, your clothes after your travels hardly permit me to invite you to the drawing room with your cousins. However, I have told your mother you are here, and when the occasion allows she will visit you with some food."

"May I speak with his mother?" said Hunter Gowan, breathing heavily.

"No."

Mr. Edward made a movement with the lamp, inviting the other man to precede him from the room. All pretense at courtesy between the two men was abandoned. Captain Hunter Gowan turned to look at me, then he left the room followed by Mr. Edward.

I could not keep that paper on me a moment longer. Gowan would have it; I had seen that in his eyes. Could I climb out of the schoolroom window? I had done it often enough in imagination during Mr. Turner's lessons. But if I made my way to the clump and delivered it to Captain Jack, I might lead his pursuers to him. I felt sure that

Gowan had his spies posted; that he had other men to do his work besides the ones I had seen. While I was turning this over in my mind I went to the window and opened it. After a moment I heard an owl cry, very close. Then the cry came again. As I looked at the dark line of the yew hedge I saw the end of it detach itself and stand apart, a shape blacker than the surrounding blackness.

I turned back to the room and took from a desk an empty china inkwell and wrapped the paper round it, praying my guess was a good one and that I knew who that figure was. I had seen him standing alone like that, on almost the same spot, the day he had sold the pup to Mr. Edward.

"Caleb?" I whispered fearfully into the dark and slowly the figure approached.

"Yes, boy?" I knew the voice at once. It was Caleb, watchful as ever.

"I have something for the Captain."

"Yes."

"I'll throw it down."

This I did, but it had not been possible quite to secure the paper and it separated itself, fluttering away to another part of the terrace while the inkwell smashed itself on the stone flags below. The sound of that, which was startling, appeared to alert no one; the figure stayed where it was for a moment, waiting, then it swooped forward like a great bird, gathered up the paper and disappeared into the trees.

Whether that paper would reach Captain Jack I could not know. I had done what I could. Reflecting that the smashed inkwell was another matter I should probably be required to explain, I settled to wait for my mother. I was very hungry.

7

A Night at the Manor

It was cold and gloomy in the schoolroom, with nothing to look at except the dark windows on one side and the piles of dusty schoolbooks on the other. In the light of the lamp the seats of our chipped and stained desks gleamed, polished by all the hours we spent sitting on them. I walked up and down between them to keep warm, clapping my arms round my shoulders as though trying to hug myself, as I had seen stonewallers do when they paused from their work on some high and windy spot.

But I did not have to wait for long. After a while I heard my mother's foot on the stairs and the clink of dishes; I went to the door and opened it for her and she came in bearing a tray full of good things. She exclaimed at the coldness of the room and bade me begin to eat at once, it would warm me; I needed no persuasion and soon, sitting at one of the desks and my mother sitting at another, I was working my way through the roast partridge she had brought. It was good to see her in the schoolroom, looking so handsome in her dark dress. She said the men were now sitting over their port and she told me who they were, giving them their styles and titles and little pieces of information about who they were descended from and connected with, which I did not follow and do not remember but these things were of great interest to my mother. It made me shy when she talked like this because I felt that an unfriendly observer, overhearing us, might feel himself permitted to smile at her eagerness. But this was the sort of life she had known as a girl and she did not have many opportunities for it now.

Her father, my grandfather, had been the owner of certain properties in Yorkshire, as my mother told me sometimes. Indeed, when she wished to marry, her father had at first opposed the match because the gentleman (who became my father) had no fortune. However, she had her way in the end, and I was always glad to be reminded that although we now lived in reduced circumstances my father could not know this, nor was it my father's fault. When he had left us we had been in a very comfortable situation, and it was precisely this richness, my mother said, which had so unsettled my father. It was only after he had gone that a series of unlucky speculations forced my grandfather to sell all he possessed; leaving him unable to look after my mother or his other children or indeed himself, for soon he died, a baffled and disappointed old gentleman. So my mother, still a young girl, with a babe of eighteen months old, who was myself, was forced to come south and be helped by Elizabeth Edward, her cousin and dear schoolroom friend, who was married to Mr. Edward, squire of Elstone, in whose house we now were. That was the story and many times my mother had told it me, bidding me be grateful and never to think hard thoughts of my father. When she looked back, she told me, she saw that my father should never have married, so restless a spirit was he, though it was just this spirit that she had loved in him. She had spun a web round him and in the end he had been right to break it, she said, for we must follow our own natures.

My mother was a generous woman, and a brave one, and I thought as I devoured the partridge and a plateful of boiled potatoes that I would wipe the smirk off the face of anyone who thought fit to smile at her pride of family. But she stopped herself in mid-account of something said by Sir Joshua Rowley (and her explanation of whom Sir Joshua Rowley was related to) and said, "Captain Hunter Gowan . . ." the smile fading from her face as she mentioned him. "You were in Cheltenham today, Frank. What for? That man told me."

"There was no time to warn you, Mother. I met a poor man—I mean a man in misfortune," I added, for I knew that my mother, though charitable, would not have approved of my becoming too deeply involved with a beggar, "and he asked me to sell something for him in the town. Joel was just leaving, so I went with him."

"But however would you have got back if Mr. Edward had not found you? I know he did because he told me so as soon as he heard Captain Hunter Gowan talking to me. Who was this man? What did he ask you to sell? Perhaps it was stolen!" she said, looking horrified. "Oh, Frank, you must be more careful! There are bad and dangerous men about. The talk at dinner quite frightened me. Terrible men have escaped from Ireland, so they say. There is even talk of invasion by the French." She gave a start. "Oh, Frank, he wasn't French, was he?"

"No, of course not, Mother. He was a gentleman, and pleasant, and needed help. So—I gave it him." I could not prevent myself feeling a little proud as I said this, for it seemed to me that I had done something difficult and useful, and I dare say this pride showed in my voice for my mother said, "How like your father you sounded then. And as secret. He wanted to change the world. Well, I think it could do with some changing." My mother looked at me for a moment and was about to say more when there was a knock at the door and her name was softly called. Then the door opened and Mrs. Edward peered in, smiling when she saw us together. She came in with another plate and a crystal glass that winked in the lamplight. "I brought Francis a piece of the gooseberry pie and a glass of claret. Surely he is old enough for a *little* claret? Oh, and in this room he needs something to warm him!"

I liked Mrs. Edward. Though she was often ill, or in her room, and I did not see her often, I was always glad when I did so. She looked warm-hearted and understanding though at times a little bewildered, as though afraid that whatever she did might displease her husband. Tonight, with her old schoolfriend and cousin, she seemed cheerful and easy and her hair hung in long curls down each side of her face—hair that on ordinary days, to be truthful, had little curl in it and hung round her pale face rather limply. Now, as she seated herself at another desk, she looked pretty and young, though not so young as my mother. I noticed she wore the necklace of yellow stones that Mr. Edward had collected for her. I quickly finished the pie and tried the wine, which tasted bitter, but it did warm me as it went down.

Both women watched me, smiling, and my mother said, "Claret with *pie*, Elizabeth? What would Sir William say!"

"A mumble of some kind of disapproval, I don't doubt. Even with his mouth full, as it has been for these last two hours! I confess I am glad he is a family connection of my husband's and not one of ours, Jane. Otherwise the expression of distaste on Mr. Edward's face would quite alarm me. As it is it makes me want to laugh! And as for the Captain that Sir William has with him . . ."

Here she was stopped by a small warning frown from my mother, who said, "Perhaps we ought not to talk so of his elders in front of Francis."

"Oh pooh, Jane! That man is a monster and so is his master—a different kind of monster. It is as well for Francis to know the world contains such grotesques. He will learn soon enough. But you've been too long away from us, Jane. I feel cruel disturbing you both, you look so contented together, but it grows very dull without you. You are so much better than I at talking about village matters with Mrs. Fowle, and Lady Rowley spends her time glaring balefully at the door, sure that Sir Joshua will enter it in an even worse state than she left him in. Bring Francis with you. Your cousins are there, Francis. They sat as quiet as mice during dinner, their ears bursting with all the great talk, and now they are bursting their stomachs with sweetmeats in the library, very dull among the ladies. They would be pleased to see you, I know. Do bring him down, Jane."

"I fear Mr. Edward was right. His appearance . . ."

Both ladies turned appraising eyes upon me, examining my boots and breeches, which I could see for myself were in a very muddy state and I dare say the rest of me was as bad.

"I do see what you mean," said Mrs. Edward. "However," she said, brightening, "it is time my boys went upstairs and I've had Sarah prepare a bed for Francis in their room. You won't mind, will you, Francis? They would so enjoy it. And your mother will stay the night with us. Heaven knows when the gentlemen will finish their port and we must be waiting for them when they do. I hope they will not have fallen out by then. I noticed a warning sign or two on Mr. Edward's brow." Here she stopped herself and giggled. "Heavens! I am really rather tipsy. How delightful! Do come, Jane, Francis; you know the room, I am sure. I'll send your cousins up directly."

Both ladies rose and my mother made to gather up the dishes but Mrs. Edward stopped her, saying, "No more work. Our work is down below," and giggled again.

"Mrs. Edward."

"Yes, Francis?"

"I dropped an inkwell out of the window. It smashed on the terrace."

"Francis!" said my mother.

"In the morning, if Mr. Turner sees . . ." I went on.

"Were you doing a trick or something?" said Mrs. Edward. "I know how it is. All those solemn questions afterwards . . . I know them too. Now let me see. It was I who furnished this room, a long time ago." She was peering into the dark cupboard at the back of the room where old books were kept, stone bottles of ink, and so on. She called to my mother to bring the lamp closer and with a little cry she reached to the back of it and brought out a new inkwell. Then she held the lamp to see which of the desks was missing one and put it into the hole. "There! Oh dear, it looks a little new, doesn't it? One moment." She reached again into the cupboard for a bottle of ink, poured some into the inkwell, dipped the tip of her finger into it and rubbed ink round the rim. "Will that serve?" she said, sucking her finger. "Oh, I remember the taste of ink so well, don't you, Jane? I shall tell Henry to sweep the terrace first thing in the morning. Come, Jane," and taking each other's arm they went out of the room like two girls.

I followed them gladly, having no wish to remain in that room any longer. Since I climbed the stairs with Captain Hunter Gowan I saw that candles had been lit in the recesses all the way down to the hall. My mother turned to kiss me good night on the landing before the two women, still linked, still whispering and laughing together, made their way down to join their guests.

I went back to fetch the lamp, for the stairs to the floor where the room of my cousins lay was still unlighted. When I found the room a good log fire was ablaze in the hearth and I was grateful for it: first I warmed my front and then I turned my back to it, watching the shadows from the fire and from my lamp dance round the high, wide room. The warmth and cheerfulness of the fire soaked into me and made me feel that by the morning I would be a match for all the Captain Hunter Gowans in the world. I thought of my mother and Mrs. Edward, and of how kind they were. I thought of Caleb out in the cold dark, but I knew that in the darkness lay many a cottage that would open gladly to his knock if he should need shelter. And I thought of the fugitive, who seemed so gay and who, now, would know he had money for his escape. But he must get away soon, for he was surrounded by enemies on the lookout for him. Not too soon, I hoped, for I longed to talk with him and find out his story. I resolved to visit the cabin as soon as I safely could but I knew I had to be careful. Captain Hunter Gowan was sure to be watching me.

Then I heard my cousins running up the stairs and I was glad.

Morgan was about my age, Thomas about a year older. Thomas sometimes tried to govern us, but without success. We could usually involve him in our schemes if only because, from his lofty point of view, he wished to see them properly conducted. But I was not really a close friend of my cousins: the brothers stuck together, as was natural, and there was a difference in our situations. Nevertheless I looked forward to sharing their room, because this had not happened for some time and it is always exciting to wake up in a strange bed with companions of your own age.

They burst into the room with their candles and were around me at once. At least, Morgan was. Thomas remembered his dignity at the last moment, checked himself, and lurked somewhat behind.

"Why were you not with us?" said Morgan. "It was such a sight, everybody jawing away and that Sir William drinking and drinking until I believed he had a chamber pot under the table and it was going in one end and coming out the other."

"Don't be disgusting," said Thomas.

I explained to them that I was too dirty.

"Well," said Morgan, politely, "you didn't miss all that much. It was rather tedious."

"Really?" said Thomas. "You are accustomed to more entertaining conversation? I didn't realize we were boring you."

"You never spoke a word," said Morgan.

"I was too concerned with listening. It would have done you good to do so too. You *were* listening. Anyway, your mouth was open."

"Well—yes," said Morgan, torn between his natural politeness to me and his desire, which I shared, to contradict his brother. "It *was* rather interesting. As well as tedious. Amazingly bloodthirsty!"

"I felt Father did not approve of that. But then, of course, he is not a soldier."

"He'd be a good one if he were," said Morgan, loyally. "Good as Captain Hunter Gowan, I'm sure of that!"

Thomas sniffed and I took the opportunity to say, "I met him," as we began to undress. "How?" they both said at once. I waited till we were at the basin that stood in the corner, dabbing our faces with water, before I told them that he had wanted to know if I had seen anything strange in High Piece last night. I said it as carelessly as I could, and climbed into my bed straight after, as though the question meant nothing to me. I wanted to learn if anything about this matter had been discussed at dinner and was afraid Thomas would turn it into a secret and say nothing.

"In what way, strange?" he said, blowing out his candle and commanding his brother to do likewise. From his voice it sounded as though he had heard no mention of it. I leaned over and put out my lamp. A log moved in the fire and flamed briefly, making the room bright and then darker than before. "I don't know," I said. "Was the subject discussed at dinner?"

"No," said Thomas, "but Ireland was. Sir William Wynne—you know he's a kinsman of ours—put down the rebellion with his own regiment. At least," Thomas added, determined to be fair, "he was one of the people who did so. Captain Hunter Gowan helped to quell it in another part, so well that Sir William has put him on his staff."

I could not help saying, "They are not proper soldiers."

"Well—no," said Thomas, his respect for truth triumphing over his pride in Sir William. "More like the ones Mr. Hicks has raised in Cheltenham. I don't suppose you have seen those," he could not help adding. "Gentlemen volunteers and loyal townspeople. They do maneuvers and drills and so on. Very fine. The Army wasn't needed in Ireland at first and Sir William's men were sent over to help the local militias—Wales isn't far from Ireland, you know?" At this point Morgan groaned at the schoolmaster tone of his brother and pretended to bury his head in his bedclothes. "They did very well," continued Thomas, ignoring him. "As well, I dare say, as what you call 'proper' soldiers. Now he wants more men because there may be more trouble. He says Welshmen and Gloucestershiremen are just the ones to keep out the French, should the French invade us from Ireland . . . I say! . . . Do you think Captain Hunter Gowan was wondering if you'd seen any *French*men round here?"

"Might there be some?" said Morgan nervously, poking his head up again from his bedclothes.

"Of course not!" said his brother scornfully. "Do you think Captain Hunter Gowan would be getting drunk, without his pistols, if there were?"

"I think Father *made* him take off those pistols," said Morgan.

"There you are then! He'd have explained to Father that he could not take them off if there'd been any danger."

"I suppose so."

We lay in silence for a while, in the dying shadows of the fire, and I began to wonder if I should learn anything more of what had passed downstairs. Morgan came to my rescue.

"It was a *bit* tedious. At first."

"You overdo that word," said his brother. "Besides, gentlemen have to talk to ladies."

"But then—when Father asked for news of events in Ireland—"

"Sir William began to tell us—" Thomas began slowly but Morgan was too full to allow his brother to hold forth again and he at once broke in.

"—about a whole crowd of rogues, thousands and thousands of them, Irishmen, murdering and piking everyone who was not of the Catholic religion—which is to say most of the gentlemen, of course—and murdering and piking them so they could steal all their property for themselves!"

"They were caught, of course. And hanged. Captain Hunter Gowan hanged some of them himself." Thomas paused. "Father appears not to care for him. I am not sure that Captain Hunter Gowan is a gentleman."

"They burned people alive in barns and threw people off bridges. The Catholics I mean," said Morgan, sounding both excited and alarmed. "He said it could happen here. Like the riots in London."

"Those were years ago," said Thomas scornfully, "before you were born. Anyway, they were *against* Catholics.

Mr. Fowle said he understood there had been excesses on both sides—"

"Captain Hunter Gowan looked as though he was going to burst at that!"

"Will you stop interrupting! Sir William Wynne said that as far as he was concerned, zeal in the putting down of rebellion was to be commended, not blamed, and Sir Joshua nodded and said, '*Canaille.*'"

"What's *canaille*?" said Morgan.

"A rabble," said Thomas. "Peasants."

"But the people in our village are peasants," I said, thinking of Joel and the boys I knew, and of Caleb.

"These are Irish peasants," said Thomas. "Savages. They have no clothes or furniture and eat only potatoes. Oh, and Captain Hunter Gowan said another thing. He said there were some English generals in the Army over there, when it came, who deserved hanging also. That didn't go down too well. He said there were officers, traitors, who were helping the rebels, trying to stop Sir William getting at them, and some generals winked an eye at this because they didn't understand the Irish situation as Sir William did. And then the captain said hanging was too good for these and I think he was about to tell us what he *would* do to them when Mother gave the signal for the ladies to rise and we never heard."

"What do you think he would do?" said Morgan and Thomas told him not to be a bloodthirsty beast. That Captain Hunter Gowan was a soldier, so it was different for him. After all, he was protecting us.

Now we fell silent, each of us with enough to think about. And soon, by the sound of my cousins' breathing, I knew they were asleep.

What had happened in Ireland sounded very terrible.

But when I thought of the peasants I knew—whom my cousins did not know, nor did any of the gentlemen round that table, of that I felt quite sure—it did not seem possible to me that they would behave in such a way unless they were driven to desperation. For who would wish to be hanged? Perhaps Irish peasants were different, being Irish, and Catholic? And was Captain Jack one of the officers who helped the rebels do these dreadful things? Above all, if the rebels were so bad, why did those Army generals "wink an eye"?

8

A Meeting in the Lane

It was too much for me, too much of a tangle, and I fell
into a sleep filled with unpleasant dreams so that when I
woke in the morning to find Sarah, the old nurse of my
cousins, rebuilding the bedroom fire, I was stiff and troubled, and my cousins seemed in the same mood. We were
all a little bad-tempered with one another at first, as
though Ireland and Captain Hunter Gowan hung over us.
But we soon cheered up when we saw that it had snowed
during the night. We ran down to the kitchen and helped
ourselves to what food we could—the cook protesting but
not really minding—and were soon out on the drive with
the sled. I kept an eye on the front door of the manor, for

my mother to appear. I knew I must return with her in case some message should come for me from Captain Jack.

After a time Mr. Edward's carriage drove up, and my mother came out of the front door and called me. I said farewell to my cousins and joined her inside the carriage to drive home. She was pale and tired after sitting up late, but seemed content. Of Captain Hunter Gowan she would hear no mention, nor say anything of the previous evening's conversation at dinner, or after it. She said she found it quite horrible, and unlike the talk of officers she had been accustomed to as a girl. What Sir William was doing in the company of such a man she could not understand. Any questions he may have put to her about me she clearly regarded, like Mr. Edward, as an impertinence, and this seemed to make her forget to ask me these questions herself. But on the whole, though sleepy, she was still gay with the effect of company, so that when the carriage dropped us at the top of our snow-covered bank and I offered to carry her down the steps, she accepted, laughing, and in that way we arrived at our cottage door.

The parlor seemed very small after the manor, and cheerless in the harsh light cast into it by the snow: the ashes of the day before yesterday were still in the grate. I was so enjoying my mother's good spirits (and so restless myself) that I said if she would go up to her room and lie on her bed I would build a fire for her there, and, yawning, she was happy to agree.

All these great events and great folk were like a holiday for us, and, I supposed it was all the army talk, my mother's thoughts seemed to run upon my father. She lay, propped on her pillows, a shawl round her shoulders and the coverlet over her feet, and told me that he had been a proper soldier; when he and his friends were together there was never any of this talk of hangings and whippings. Though he had told her often that he had been present at another rebellion when he was a very young ensign, that of our Colonies in America, and he always said it was the worst work he ever did, because he sympathized with their cause. "It changed them all, that American war," she said. "All the best ones. I think that was why they were beaten. But of course a soldier must always do his duty." She stared, smiling, at the wall, and I knelt at the fire with the bellows, hardly daring to use them in case I distracted her and stopped her talking, for I had not heard her talk quite in this way about my father. "I think from that time on he wanted to leave the Army. But soldiering was all he knew, and he had no fortune but his pay. This might not have mattered to him had I not come along." She smiled. "He could withstand an enemy but he couldn't withstand a girl who had set her heart on him! I was shameless, poor man. . . . He loved us, you know, Francis, that was the worst of it. I suffered, but so did he. Do not marry, Francis, till you know you are no longer restless. A person must be restless on their own. I knew nothing . . . Now pass me my book. This is really very nice. You're a good boy . . . And no more visits to Cheltenham without telling me. Have you any more to say about that?"

"It's over, Mother. I helped this man and we'll hear no more."

"I suppose not . . ." She looked at me. "Stay near the house today though, would you? I might sleep."

I promised I would not go too far away, and she settled to her reading. I was grateful to her for not asking me more questions, for I had guessed from her face that she wanted to.

I went outside in the snow and kicked about in it a little, feeling listless and disappointed, because so much had happened in the last twenty-four hours that my ordinary life seemed stale. I did not know what next to do about the fugitive. Perhaps nothing; perhaps he had already gone.

Turning all this over, rather sulkily, in my mind, I found that without my meaning it my steps had taken me to the top of the bank, to the woodshed bordering the lane. From there I looked across and down into the copse where Captain Jack lay, and saw that there was no chance of going to see him, because the snow lay unbroken and my steps would have shown. As I stared down, noticing the snow was indeed unbroken, and therefore he must be inside the hut unless he had left it before the snow began to fall, I became aware that I was not alone.

On a small rise in the lane and on an enormous horse, sat Captain Hunter Gowan. He was peering about him, standing up in his stirrups the better to do so, glancing down at the copse and the woods that lay below it, and then, in the other direction, down at our cottage which he could not see among the trees, but he could see the wisps of smoke, very blue among the white and black of the snow-covered branches, that came from my mother's bedroom fire.

What he saw seemed to satisfy him, or he seemed to lose interest after a few moments, for then I saw him, as I shrank back into the cover of the trees, perform a most extraordinary series of military exercises. Huge pistols were stuck in a belt fastened round his greatcoat, and also attached to the belt was a long curved sword. This he drew, and began whirling about his head and slashing down at imaginary foes, saying Ha! Ha! with each swing as though a head rolled at every blow.

He clearly believed himself to be unobserved, and I could imagine no real soldier behaving like this by himself on a lonely road. Then he clumsily spurred his great horse into a gallop, somewhat burdened by all the weapons he had about him, and sped down the lane, huzzaing and slashing, cutting and thrusting, the brim of his hat pushed absurdly back by the speed of his passage, until he disappeared. I hardly had time to consider this strange spectacle before he reappeared from the opposite direction, doing the same and bearing down upon the part of the lane where I stood partly hidden. I scorned to hide from him any more, for I already hated him; and his solitary playing at the cavalry captain—playing it as even I could see very badly—made him ridiculous in my eyes. He could barely stay on his horse.

If he was absurd in my eyes, his own, which bulged always, protruded even more when he saw me as he galloped past, and he kept them fixed on me, turning his head over his shoulder as he attempted to rein in his horse. Some way past he managed this and turned, coming back to me.

When he drew abreast he stopped, panting, and took some moments to gather himself.

"That's how we deal with them! Traitors!" he growled and swung his sword past my face, a good distance from it. "Felt the wind of that, did you? Snip! Off come your fingers!" And he swung again, again at a safe distance from my body, for he seemed to have no very certain control of his sword; although there was no denying the force with which it passed through the air. "There!" he said, making a mime of fixing something to the point of it. "A

Croppie finger on the tip of me blade. An excellent thing
to stir a lady's punchbowl! Ha! I did that once!" He
offered the "finger" to me. "Take it!

"What?" he went on, when I made no move. "Shrink
from a Croppie finger? That hand'll never hold a pike—
d'ye see? Know what a Croppie is? No. You know nothing
in England, and we save England for you! They crop
their hair short, the damned Papists, to show their sympa-
thies with the king murderers in France. You know
what'll happen if they win? We'll be burned in our beds
by a starving rabble! You too—and your fine Mr. Edward!
And Englishmen complain we're being too hard on the ig-
norant swine while we do England's dirty work for them!
Bah! My militia made mincemeat of them—like this!—like
this!" Here he began slashing the air again, his yellow
eyes popping from his face with the exertion. "And Sir
William's Welshmen too, oh by God, yes! Then the British Army comes and says, 'Oh no no no *no*'"—here he
mimicked refined English tones—"'Oh no, yew must *tray*
the dear fellows first, get evidence written out in books
one mile high, respect the law, yew kneow.' The law my
arse! You should hear what my loyal Catholics say to that,
and see what *they* do to their murdering cousins! There's
been one round here. He slipped us. I'll have him. He'll
not be far." He threw back his head and looked down at
me through narrowed eyes, using his finicking accent
again. "*Yew* have seen nay one, *of course!*"

"What did he look like, sir?"

"There are so many strangers round here you need a
description?" He had gone very still and after a pause he
said softly, "I don't trust you, boy." Then he appeared to
lose interest, as though I was beneath his contempt.
"How the devil should I know what he looked like! Rats

don't show their faces by day. My men will know him soon enough."

"You—said you had captured him and he had slipped you."

"My men had him. He or another. It makes no matter, they should all hang. You don't like what I say? Neither does your uncle, or whatever the blazes he is. Sir William Wynne likes what I say. And the work I can do with this!" He fell to brandishing his sword again and had he not been in such earnest I should have laughed. He was more than half mad but entirely dangerous.

He wished to terrify me, and soon he would have done so, had not his horse, as soon as the sword began to wave, remembered its military duties; or perhaps Captain Gowan set his spurs to it accidentally; at all events he left me with such abruptness he was hurled backwards in the saddle as the horse leapt forward, and it was a long moment before he was able to right himself, in mid-gallop, and set to his swinging and slashing once more as he disappeared from sight. The way he was going it would not be long before he came in sight of the trees that surrounded the manor, and I guessed he would slow down and sheathe his sword before Mr. Edward could put his cool eyes upon him. What Mr. Edward would have thought of his horsemanship and his antics made me smile to consider. Though for some, I guessed, Captain Hunter Gowan had been no smiling matter.

I stared down again at the copse and thought of the hunted creature probably still hidden there, so much nobler, it seemed to me, than his pursuer. It was difficult to believe that the one was astride a great horse, in a yellow coat with pistols stuck in his belt and a black hat crammed over his stiff red hair, while the other was ill, alone, injured and in fear of his life. I saw a figure come out of the wood below the copse, the wood that lined the river where lay most of the village, pause as though watchful, then make its way along the edge of the trees up towards the lane. For a moment I hoped it was Captain Jack, because I so much wanted to see him. But soon I knew it was Caleb Bawcombe, which was nearly as good. He would surely have news.

I waited where I was, and when he at last reached the lane I stepped forward and made to greet him. I saw no change in his expression, so I stopped, expecting him to do so too. But he did not, merely nodded and touched his woollen cap, continuing on his way, his figure brown as a piece of earth against the white of the lane.

My cheeks burned. It was perhaps because of me that the Captain was still alive—yet I was to be allowed no part in this business! Caleb's eyes had told me that I was a cub who belonged to the manor.

I walked down the steps to the cottage. They would have me belong nowhere. Well, I did not care. At least I belonged to myself, and if I lived I should find Captain Jack, help him, learn his story and have some place in the aloneness that surrounded him. For he also appeared to belong nowhere.

9

Caleb's Cottage

By the next afternoon the snow had thawed so much it lay in streaks on the ground, and there was little danger of leaving tracks. So, going down to the village and making my way *up* to the copse so that I could not be overlooked from the lane, I went to visit Captain Jack in his hut.

There was no one there. Nor was there any sign that anyone had ever been there. The place was tidier than I had seen it, a smoothed blanket on the bunk, fresh logs neatly piled by the stove, and on top of it, burnished and ready for use, my mother's fry pan. This I had forgotten, and picked it up to carry home.

Looking back, I wonder if my mother guessed that something was going on. She asked me no questions, about the pan or anything else, but in the days that followed I was so moody she must have noticed something. I took opportunities to quarrel with her, then I would fling out of the house and go walking among bare trees that shifted and sighed as though they were as disappointed as I was. At fifteen years old I felt life had touched me and had now moved on.

At my lessons I was inattentive but Mr. Turner hardly noticed, he was so impressed and flustered by the great company and by all the comings and goings: Mr. Edward did much entertaining at this time to amuse his guests, who gave no sign of intention to depart. There were fewer lessons anyway, because my cousins were called out to go riding or take part in a shoot on the estate. I dare say sometimes I would have been allowed to join them, but it suited my sulky humor to remain on my own. I was forever on the lookout for some message or signal from the Captain, but the days passed and none came.

I did allow myself, however, to follow the beagle pack as they chased after hares, and so was able to observe again the extraordinary Sir William Wynne and the even more eccentric, lunatic, Hunter Gowan.

Sir William, only a little more soberly attired in the open fields than he had been on the night of the dinner, was, despite his vast bulk, strangely nimble. On his small feet in their high leather boots he seemed always able to position himself well for the sight of the hounds, and to be able to guess the next turn of the hare. I guessed that he was a more formidable soldier than he appeared. More often than not he was in at the kill. Exhorting the hounds he would grow empurpled, and with Hunter Gowan yelping like a hound himself they gave the impression that master and man—for it was very clear that Sir William was Hunter Gowan's master—were hard put to it not to fall upon the hare themselves and tear it to pieces with their own teeth.

Mr. Edward, or so I felt, for I watched everything carefully in case something to do with Captain Jack should come to my notice, found it each day more hard to disguise his deep displeasure with the behavior of Hunter Gowan, and his impatience with his kinsman Sir William. They brought to our country sports a savagery and a tenacity that made these pastimes for the first time distasteful. I was heartily sorry for any enemy they might find who was weaker than they. The smallness and feebleness of the foe—in this case the hare—did nothing to diminish their ferocity, and it was not the chase that gave them the most excitement but, too clearly, the death. If this was the sort of men soldiers were, or the way soldiers became, I was ashamed of the profession of my father. But I did not believe all soldiers were like that.

On the seventh night after my stay at the manor I resolved, come what may, whatever unmannerly rebuff I might receive, to knock on the door of Caleb's cottage. There I would ask him, and not leave him until I had some satisfaction, what had happened to the Note of Hand I had passed him, and what had happened to Captain Jack.

As I have said, relations between myself and my mother were not good at this time because of the fit of disappointment that had settled upon me, and more than once I had stayed out of the house very late. My mother had more or less come to accept this as part of my bad temper and her acceptance made my plan easier to effect.

That evening, before dusk, I told her that I was going for a long walk and she was not to stay supper for me. She nodded, saying nothing, and bent over her sewing with such patience that I longed to tell her the whole of my story. But I dared not, for she might feel impelled to tell others when she knew, and the little knowledge that I had might prove dangerous both to her and to the Captain. So, miserably enough, but as I thought in true manly fashion, I marched out of the house, up the steps and down across the field.

As I crossed it my manliness faltered somewhat: the copse was still haunted for me by the faces of villains and the sight of the body hanging. When I recalled the fear I had experienced when a hand came from behind and covered my mouth, I nearly turned round and ran home. For the owner of that hand was the man I was now going to see.

I found myself trying not to hope that he would be away from home. Between the world of the manor and the world of the village there was little connection. Mr. Edward owned the village, and though I believed he was not a hard or grasping landlord, he incurred all the resentments that such a position brings. I had heard murmurs against him: about thatch left unmended while rains spoiled the few furnishings beneath it, about expectation of labor in foul weather, about the behavior of his pack of hounds among the vegetables in their small gardens. Mr. Edward, I heard, always made good these losses, but his cool manner was mistaken for haughtiness, and it did indeed betray a sense I knew he had, that these people were not quite of the same clay as himself.

I might have thought so too, were it not for my position, suspended as it were between the two worlds. But although my village friends hardly bothered to guard their tongues in front of me, they did not take me fully into their confidence either. To them I belonged more to the world of the manor than I did to theirs. And this, whether I liked it or not, was true.

To Caleb, then, I was one of the people to whom he was, in his stealthy way, a sworn foe. When he opened his door and saw me he would look at me with that cold and guarded eye of his—not altogether different from the eye with which Mr. Edward habitually regarded me: and it was therefore with a quaking heart, and feeling not for the first time a little sorry for myself, that I found myself standing in the near-darkness outside his cottage.

It was one of a row of joined cottages on the bank of our little river. Most of the others in the row were lived in by his brothers or by friendly neighbors. Indeed there was no one in the village who dared be unfriendly to the Bawcombes, for together they made a powerful family. Nor were there many who would wish to be, for they were an openhearted and generous clan, given to quarreling and fighting and drinking, but skilled workmen, and such faults were not those that disrecommend a man in the eyes of country people.

In Caleb's cottage there were lights and the sound of company.

It cost me much to raise my hand to knock. But I told myself that unless I did so I could give up all hope of ever finding out what had happened to Captain Jack. So I raised my cold knuckles, and at last gave the wood a longer and more commanding rap than I had intended.

All sound within the cottage ceased. Nothing could have dismayed me more. Then a dog began to bark and was silenced with a curse and a thump.

I knocked again, more carefully, my heart knocking as loud, and at last the door moved, but only a crack, and a woman put her face to it. I recognized her as one of the family, though whether a wife or a sister I could not remember. "I have come to see Caleb—please," I said. She shut the door and behind it I heard murmurs. I wanted to turn and run, perhaps I was on the point of doing so when the door opened again, more fully this time, and the doorway was entirely filled by the large form of Caleb, in his shirt, looking down at me.

"I—came to see if you got the paper," I said.

"I did," said Caleb, paying attention to the tobacco he was stuffing into a short pipe.

"And if it reached its destination?"

"It did," he said, sticking the pipe in his mouth and looking at me as if that closed the matter.

I was angry now. I had found Captain Jack at the end of a rope. I had sold his cross. I deserved better than this. "If you think I am a spy, I am not! I am as much concerned in this business as you are, and would no more think of telling that man—the one who shot at you—than I would . . ."

Before I could think of a comparison, Caleb looking at me unmoved, a voice came from behind him, "Who is it, Caleb?" and there was the sound of a chair being pushed back.

Caleb grunted to himself, with annoyance I thought, and continued to block the doorway while the same voice said, from closer behind him, "It sounds like someone I remember, or think I remember. Am I to be permitted to see who it is?"

"'Tis the lad who cut you down from the tree," said

Caleb, not moving, and continuing to look speculatively at me.

"Then I must ask you to invite him into your house, for here is a boy to whom I owe some thanks."

Reluctantly, grunting again, Caleb pressed against the doorjamb and with a jerk of his hand gestured me past him. Immediately there was a small pack of dogs around my ankles, and cries from the room for them to be still. I blinked in the light, for my interview with Caleb had taken place in the near-dark. I soon saw there were many people in the room, all with their eyes upon me.

But mine were only for the figure who retreated in front of me. He was dressed in a loose white shirt of some fine cloth, there was lace at his wrists and a high scarf of green about his neck. He turned, a smile on his face, and it was Captain Jack.

But how transformed! He was dressed like a dandy, the color was back in his dark face, and his short black hair that a few days before the rain and mud had fastened so tight to his skull was now black and crisp, though there were flecks of gray in it. He was a little above medium height, sparely built, and looked at me with great friendliness.

He stepped towards me, hands outstretched, and taking both my hands in his, he said, "That was a good deed you did me that night. It was good, very good, for a boy your age to sell my cross so well, God forgive me! But you see," he went on, relinquishing my hands and stretching his arms out for admiration, "you see what I did with a few of those guineas? Do you recognize me?"

"There are people who still search for you, sir. If you have the money now, should you not be gone?"

"We have only just met!" he exclaimed, laughing. "I

am safe with Caleb and these friends." Here he looked round, and received smiles in return. "Soldiers will not be sent for me here, and no one else dare come!" There were sounds of agreement at this, and laughter.

"Soldiers!" I said, startled. "Surely you are not an enemy of England!"

"No, no, no. No enemy at all! But—tell me," he said, his head on one side. "Did I not meet a shepherd lad? You are no shepherd."

"He's from the manor," said Caleb.

"A son of Mr. Edward?" said Captain Jack. "Then why did you pretend otherwise?" He was still smiling, but he required an answer.

I was grateful to be rescued by Caleb. "I dare say till he knew who *you* were he didn't want you to know who *he* was," he said.

The Captain looked at me with interest. "That was quick. A lump of a near-dead man on your hands and the clap of Caleb's great paw over your face—he told me of that!—and still you used your headpiece! So, a son of Mr. Edward."

"No, sir, a distant kinsman. Nor am I of the manor, though I take my schooling there with my cousins. I live in a cottage with my mother, near where you . . . where I found—"

"A distant kinsman? You are called Francis, am I right? May I have the honor of your other name?"

"Francis Place, sir."

Hereupon Captain Jack behaved in an extraordinary manner.

10

Captain Jack Again

His expression changed not at all. There was still the delighted smile that had mockery in it, but as though he mocked himself. He still seemed perfectly at ease, but a moment after I had spoken my name his gaze shifted to Caleb and then, with little jerks of his neck, to the faces of other people in the room. His eyes rested on each until a move of his neck directed his eyes to the next. But he appeared not to be looking at them; at least, not as he had looked so slowly, one after the other, at his executioners. This quick glancing seemed to be a way he had of settling his thoughts. When they had accomplished the circuit of the room his eyes returned to mine and he laughed.

"Well, that is a fine name, good as any other. Come, let us continue our game," turning to a small table at which sat Hiram, one of Caleb's brothers, with a leather dice cup in his hand.

"Please," I said, before he could sit. "I have told you my name. May I have yours?"

He continued to seat himself, then he turned to look at me, taking the dice cup from Hiram and shaking it. "I like your directness. In Ireland they call me Captain Moonlight. We have a taste for such names in Ireland. There is a gang called the Peep O'Day Boys—is that not fine?" He fingered his green stock, raising his eyebrows comically at me. "Here they call me Scarf Jack. I'm not sure I don't like that better. Come!" And he threw the dice. "May the boy be seated, Caleb?" he said, bending to look at the dice.

"Here," said Caleb, his pipe alight by now. He drew me up a wooden box to sit on, and seated himself on another by my side.

There were two settles of wood, with high backs, on each side of a black oven set into the chimney. One part of the oven was an open grate in which there was a very hot fire, and each of the settles was crowded with Bawcombes of all ages. Daniel, Caleb's son, was among them, but though he smiled at me he seemed content to copy the manner of the rest, which was to take small notice of me, or none. I sat with Caleb near the end of one settle and at the other end, nearest the fire, a young girl with red cheeks suckled a baby who bawled when she moved him from one breast to the other. Next to her was a male Bawcombe, her husband I supposed, who was carefully sewing three large pieces of leather, like aprons, one on top of the other. Next to him sat a large boy whom I knew as

Mustard, though I never knew why he was called that, whose job it was tonight to prevent with his boots a fat crawling baby from making his way to the fire and reaching up at the bars. He made a sport of it, and the baby appeared to enjoy it also. On the other settle was a similar scene, male, female and infantile, partly obscured by smoke from lamps and pipes, and although my impression at first had been of a great disorder it was not long before I began to compare this cheerful scene favorably with the sort of life I sometime shared at the manor. I drank it in eagerly enough, sitting next to Caleb who did not speak but puffed upon his pipe. When the others talked I sometimes could not understand what they said because their Gloucestershire was more broad than I could interpret. There were jokes at which the whole company laughed whereas I had not been able to catch one word.

I became conscious that the Captain, apparently intent on his game with Hiram, was sometimes casting glances in my direction; to save the embarrassment of our eyes too often meeting I attempted to engage Caleb in conversation. I felt sure his guest in the scarf had told Caleb at least a part of his tale and that Caleb approved, otherwise he would not have taken the risk of giving him shelter under the noses of his pursuers. I determined to try and open up that tight-shut oyster, Caleb.

I had hopes I would be assisted in this attempt by the cider jug which circulated freely, even the infants partaking, and my hopes rose higher when Caleb commanded that I should be given a mug and the mug filled.

I drank, imitating the hearty action of the others, nearly burying my face in the good apple smell of the mug, and as I emerged I remarked to Caleb, as easily as I could, talking of the news that was on everyone's lips at this time, "Things look bad then, in Ireland?"

"Seems so," said Caleb.

"What's the trouble?"

"Landlord–tenant trouble, *he* tells me." Caleb jerked his head to where the Captain sat engrossed, and then returned to his contemplation of the fire.

"And our Army is putting it down?"

"The Captain says the landlords theyselves is putting it down, pretty hard too, with armies of their own, militia and such. Captain says the Army would like to put the *landlords* down but they dursn't because of the government."

"But what has the Captain to do with this, and who were the men who tried to kill him?"

"Reckon they was in the pay o' the landlords over there and the Captain was getting too hot for 'em."

"But why here? I mean—why should they try to hang him in the copse on High Piece? Why not in Ireland?"

"You'd better ask *him.* They had their reasons, I dare say. Mightn't have been a boy in Ireland to cut him down," said Caleb, with the nearest approach to a smile that he ever favored me with. Perhaps my drinking of the cider had pleased him.

"I *shall* ask him, Caleb, and I hope he will tell me. I wonder why he stays here, though."

Caleb laughed now, with pleasure. "There's a man he wants afore he goes. He won't go till he has him and he has my blessing on that."

Now the man at the table, who had been observing this conversation, as I felt certain he observed all that passed around him, called across, "What do you think of the company at the manor, Francis?"

"Very little, sir," I said.

"Tell me their names again."

"Sir William Wynne—"

"There's many a poor man in Ulster would see *him* in Hell, and his Welsh regiment with him. They call themselves The Ancient Britons and do our woad-covered ancestors great wrong."

"I heard he was a brave soldier."

"If to shoot and roast a pheasant be brave. Faced by old men and children he's a Hercules . . . Who else d'you have up there?"

"Captain Hunter Gowan—"

"*Captain!*" He roared this so loud that a hush fell on the company. "*Captain!* A thief-taker from the Wicklow hills turned magistrate so he could flog and burn and make rebels of men who'd never have thought of it else. What army was he ever captain in except that of his own mad dogs? Before God, it makes me ill to think of it! Sir William Wynne make a captain of *him*?" He paused and collected himself. "It doesn't surprise me. Nothing does . . . Lionel! Give a tune on your fiddle." So saying he rose from his chair and put on a beautiful blue coat of velvet which was lying in a corner. As he lifted it I saw a pistol lying beneath, ready to his hand. Then, as the fiddle began, he bowed ceremoniously to the prettiest girl in the room, she who had been shortly before feeding her infant. The invitation put more red in her cheeks even than the fire, but she rose to join him and they began a gentle jig in the small space between the two settles. Another couple followed suit and the rest of us clapped the beat except for Caleb who looked on, occasionally waving his pipe to the rhythm of the tune.

Now the room began to sway and tilt around me and I

greatly feared I was going to be sick. The heat of the
fire, the stuffiness and the music all worked upon me.
Although I dare say it was the cider that had done the
greatest damage, with its deceptive sweetness, and out of
sheer nervousness I had been dipping my face into my
mug more than was wise.

The music came to an end amid laughter and clapping
and calls for more. But my appearance, even at that distance, was of a kind to make Scarf Jack step towards me
and raise me from my box. "This lad needs air. It's your
good cider, Lionel," and there was more laughter because, I guess, such sufferers were not rare at their gath-
erings.

Caleb laid a hand on Scarf Jack's arm. "Let one of the
others take him. 'Tis not safe for you out there."

"I shall keep to the wood by the river, have no fear.
This lad needs a good sousing. Besides, I owe him a
rescue."

I sensed, even through my misery, that Caleb was still
uncertain because he muttered something, but it was
clear that Captain Jack had determined to take charge of
me. I felt his arm about my shoulders, and even after he
had raised me I still had the sensation of my brain trying
to batter its way through the top of my head. Soon I
found myself supported by him outside the cottage and
heard the fiddle strike up once more.

"This way, Francis," he said, and led me through trees
to the river. Stooping, he gathered water in his hands and
splashed it in my face and on the back of my neck, making me bend forward. The cold water on the top of my
backbone revived me wonderfully and I told him so.

"A wet collar never hurt a man," he said, and for the

first time for a while, I felt to my relief that I was not to undergo the humiliation of being sick.

"Sit down now, and don't shut your eyes. I know very well about such matters, you see," he said, and laughed. "Here, I'll sit beside you."

So at last we were seated together side by side on a fallen willow, this strange man and myself, both of us gazing down at the black, moving waters of our winter river, the dark trees behind our heads. The clouds raced past the newly risen moon and the clouds of befuddlement slowly eased from my brain.

But I knew this was my chance to clear my mind in other ways as well. "Sir, why did those men want to kill you *here*?"

I felt he was on his guard, though whether against me or against his other enemies I could not tell. Perhaps being watchful had become his nature. "The strangest, strangest chance—Ssh!"

He rose slowly to his feet and turned to face the trees. I made some movement for though I strained my ears I heard nothing, but he gripped my arm so hard I almost called out. In his right hand was the pistol.

Still I could hear nothing except the gurgling sound of the river and the noise of a light breeze in the branches above us. Somewhere in the distance I heard the bleating of a sheep. Then, sure enough, a twig cracked and the Captain said softly into the dark, "Step out and let us see you." There were more cracks of undergrowth now, and the sound of clothing, and a figure stepped from among the tree trunks. Captain Jack kept his pistol very still and said, "Come forward with your arms raised." The figure obeyed and said, "It's only me, Captain. Lionel," and when it did indeed turn out to be the rather shambling

Lionel Bawcombe, Captain Jack did not at once lower his
pistol but said, "Why are you following us?" and Lionel
told him Caleb had instructed him to do so, in case the
Captain met with any enemies.

"Very well, Lionel, you may now return. Thank Caleb
from me for his concern, and tell him I will be back, as I
told him, within ten minutes." When Lionel moved off
through the little wood, making much more noise this
time, Captain Jack remained staring after him and I
heard him say, "He was quiet, by God!"

He had indeed been quiet, and I blushed to think how
I had prided myself on my eyes and ears, when I, unlike
my companion, had heard nothing. He was still staring
into the dark. His body did not relax its attitude of attention until, at the edge of the trees, the unmistakable
figure of Lionel at last emerged, made for the cottage and
stepped in. We heard the door close behind him. Still he
waited, whistling between his teeth, watching, and then,
with a small "Humph!" he turned and resumed his place
beside me on the fallen tree.

"The strangest chance indeed," he continued, as though
we had not been interrupted. "I knew Sir William was a
kinsman of Mr. Edward—of whom I also know something
—but that Wynne should have been recruiting his
damned regiment through this county and have reached
this point—no, that is very strange . . ." He sighed, and
appeared to gather his thoughts. "Francis—Wynne and
Gowan are two of the bloodiest rogues in Ireland. They
had reasons for wishing me dead, but out of the country,
I had too many friends there and they were already in
trouble, they'd gone too far too often. So I guess they
paid that bunch of cutthroats to follow me to Bristol and
hang me where their masters could inspect the work. If

I'd been found before they could cut me down and bury me somewhere, who could blame it on Wynne, a mile away and dining with his cousin?"

"Word must have got to Gowan. He came down to the oak next morning."

"And decided to shoot the good Caleb instead! He would have shot God Himself that day."

"But why didn't they kill you in battle—in Ireland?"

"They couldn't catch me!" I heard, rather than saw, his smile. "I'm not too bad a soldier, Francis. And they couldn't murder me because the Army would have known who was to blame. And I mean the Army, not that gang of floggers and burners that Gowan pretends to lead. There are still men who want Ireland made peaceful, not destroyed entirely. The Army had Gowan weighed up at last. Too late. They arrested him for cruelties on my evidence but they had to let him go. Witnesses were bribed, big names were involved. It was then I decided to go for other help. So I sailed."

"Help in London? Are there others like you?"

"Some." His answer was so short I felt I was touching on dangerous ground. He went on, "I was drunk in Bristol. Like you are, you young devil! I made three of them drunker than I was. But there was a fourth—waiting. Feller with black eyebrows. See him that night? I'll find him . . ."

"But you were caught before."

"When?"

"Your back."

"I was telling a village Gowan's militia was on its way in a burning mood. The militia arrived too soon, I pretended to be a villager and suffered the fate of the rest."

"Were all that village rebels?"

"Not till Gowan came. After that they were rebels, sure enough."

"Was it bad? Being flogged?"

"You want to kill the man who orders it."

"So you are staying to kill Gowan?"

"I have to."

We were silent for a moment and then I dared to say what was in my mind. "But isn't that—murder?"

"Call it so." He held his right hand out so that it was outlined against the black of the water. "See that? It's black with blood. Never be a soldier, Francis. It kills the heart in you. Just now I could have put a ball through Lionel as easy as I'd kill a rabbit. You get used to it. I could kill you."

I stared at his hand horrified. There was such a cruel indifference in his voice. "You would have me do it fair with Gowan?" he said. "Very well. I shall. I must not make you ashamed of me. But you will have to help."

"Oh yes," I said. "But will he have a chance?"

"To kill me?"

"I mean—to escape."

"And do more murders? I wonder if you know what you mean. But you will help?"

"As long as my mother has nothing to fear."

"Your mother shall have nothing to do with it." He was sharp. "Get word to me next time Mr. Gowan plans to go riding in company. Mind that. He must not be alone."

"But they will be too many for you!"

"No chance of that!" Then his mood changed and he said bitterly, "My work is done. Or undone. These last months will poison Ireland for a hundred years. I'm fit for nothing but killing and being killed. I sicken myself!" He stood up, dusting himself behind. "And my breeches are spoiled. Your Cheltenham tailors worked fast but they know how to make out a bill! Shouldn't you be rejoining your mother? She must be proud of you."

"I have told her nothing."

He seemed to examine me in the darkness and then grunted. "Well—I must be rejoining my friends anyway. It's odd. I want you to think well of me. But not of the way I live. Never that."

"Is there nothing fine in it?"

"Not often." He held out his hand to me, the one he had told me had caused so many deaths. I took it gladly because his aloneness—and I was ashamed of the thought at once, for what comparison could there be between us? —was something like my own.

11

The Challenge

Very soon I had the information for Captain Jack.

The day after our conversation by the river, the manor was filled with preparations for the fox hunt which was to take place the next day. This was to be a large affair, the largest of the season, and the meet was to be at the Frogmill Inn, some miles from our village. Riders were to converge on that place from all parts of our county and Mr. Edward, still endeavoring to entertain his guests though never a keen huntsman himself, had decided to lead a party to join it. A mount had been found for me, and if this other business had not been so much in my mind, I would have rejoiced with my cousins that we were to go hunting together.

The meet was to be at ten o'clock, which meant we would have to leave the manor an hour before, and so here was a perfect opportunity for Scarf Jack to encounter Hunter Gowan "in company," as he had specified.

This news I passed to Lionel Bawcombe, whom I found repairing a piece of collapsed wall just outside the manor gate. I did so by saying merely, "Scarf Jack. Nine o'clock. This lane. Tomorrow," while I walked past him, without turning my head. I would have found this method of communicating ridiculous if I had not been taught it by Caleb, and if I had not been sure that the whole business was deadly serious. I had time to see him slightly nod, and considered the message as good as delivered: though not without misgivings, for it was obvious that Captain Jack did not trust Lionel. However, I did not see how that piece of news, which he had asked for, could be used to his harm, and I had already decided that it was much too dangerous for me to risk being seen at Caleb's cottage.

I knew that matters had to be brought to a head quickly. It was clear that Mr. Edward's guests were not going to quit the village until they had news of Scarf Jack one way or the other. They would have their spies out—I had observed members of the gang I had seen in town coming to report—and it must be only a matter of time before he was discovered. My cousins told me that Sir William Wynne had let their father know that he wished to stay until his recruiting was finished, and that the men who came to confer with him were giving him information of their success. I was sure they were reporting failure to find Scarf Jack. Morgan told me that his father's face, when he caught sight of one of these men lurking in the kitchen courtyard, had been comical to see, but that Sir William had not appeared to notice.

Both my cousins believed that Sir William noticed very little, but I was not so sure. I remembered his extraordinary skill when out with the beagles, and even in domestic matters he seemed to know very well what he was about. He sailed about the manor on his little feet in their exquisite shoes like a huge, gaudily painted ship. He did indeed seem to sail, slowly, because his head did not go up and down as he stepped but always kept on the same level, like the crow's nest of a ship in smooth water. He said little but "Ho!" and "Hum!" while others spoke, leaving his own view of any matter to be expressed by Hunter Gowan. But I believed that very little escaped him. Once I glimpsed him on his smooth passage to the library. He gave the impression of utmost vagueness. But I saw through the open doors that he arrived there precisely in time to achieve the best chair and the first cup of tea.

On the morning of the hunt he was astride a big chestnut gelding, and although a spectator might have felt tempted to laugh at the sight of a fatness that seemed too great even for so large a horse, it was clear, though he did very little, that he was in command of his mount. One had to look away from him, however, for fear of being dazzled. He wore a pink coat of military cut, dark green breeches, a sash of blue and a three-cornered hat of a purplish color. Hunter Gowan was in his usual yellowish brown, Mr. Edward in black, my cousins and myself and what servants stood about were in various drab shades, so that Sir William was like a rainbow in our midst. It seemed that the warlike pursuits of Sir William and Hunter Gowan had given them both a taste for fancy dress; for though, as I have said, Gowan dressed simply enough, as we assembled he still wore his brace of pistols and his cavalry sword.

Before we moved off Mr. Edward asked him to remove
these weapons and hand them to a servant. Hunter
Gowan refused, whereupon Mr. Edward said that he re-
gretted he was unable to invite him to be of the company.
The two men stared at each other, and my cousins and I
held our breath while we heard their father defied. A
hush fell on the company, the only sound the horses shaking their heads as they adjusted the bits in their mouths,
and no one moved; except for Sir William, who took snuff
and made one or two of those noises that passed in him
for conversation. Perhaps in this way some communi-
cation was made to Hunter Gowan, for after looking
at Sir William, he suddenly flung his pistols at a servant
who was standing by and he only just managed to catch
them. They were followed by the sword, which the servant allowed to clatter to the ground. Mr. Edward turned
his horse's head and we started along the drive.

It was a perfect morning. A little too bright perhaps,
but there was just enough movement in the air to carry
the scent, and there was not a cloud to spoil the slightly
misty blue sky. I cursed Hunter Gowan for beginning the
day so badly, leaving us all shaken and distracted. I almost found it in myself to wish Captain Jack a million
miles away too, so I could enjoy my day in peace, for I
dearly loved hunting.

What began badly continued so. Our quiet progress
along the drive did not suit the high spirits or ill temper
of Mr. Hunter Gowan. He curvetted and pranced, led us
and turned back to us, and then, riding with long stirrups
and seated well back in the saddle, his feet sticking out
in front of him, he galloped away to the gates with a
whoop, so that I thought he would exhaust his horse before it even reached the meet. At the gates he reined in

and awaited us, his horse prancing. Mr. Edward led us on at an even pace as though Gowan did not exist. When at last we reached him, Gowan again spurred his horse to a gallop, leapt through the open gates, and when we next saw him was going full tilt along the lane in the direction of another rider who was proceeding slowly towards us, very erect in the saddle. There was no chance of their passing, they were sure to coincide at the narrowest part of the lane and the stranger was in the very middle of it. To our horror we saw Gowan, instead of slowing, put his spurs to his horse in an attempt to ride the man down, and the other seemed unaware of his approach.

There was nothing we could do but watch and wonder how the approaching rider could get out of the way in time. He continued, oblivious of his danger: appeared to be savoring the morning and the prospect from the high lane. Then, as Gowan was nearly upon him, instead of trying to scramble up the bank out of his way he did the opposite. Apparently having seen or heard nothing of any horseman coming his way, he turned his own horse directly across the lane and sat, reins slack, admiring the view.

Gowan was unable to ride straight through him, and we heard him scream with anger as he reined his horse so abruptly that he nearly slid over its tail. He continued to shout at the other horseman and Mr. Edward quickened his pace. We all did the same and arrived to find Gowan, his yellow face covered with even more blotches, bellowing at the top of his lungs, "*Will* you get out of my way, sir!"

The man he was yelling at was Captain Jack. Almost from the first I had guessed this, though I had not seen him before on a horse. And the view he was contem-

plating was nicely chosen: it was the copse and the old
oak.

I had not seen Captain Jack looking so splendid, either.
He was dressed in his blue velvet coat which by day was
even finer than I remembered, and wore a tall felt hat of
blue with a cockade or rosette at the side of it in the same
material. He sat his horse with perfect calmness as though
it was the most natural thing in the world to find himself
confronted by the incensed Gowan. "You are overheated,
sir," was all he said to that gentleman and then, to us, as
we arrived on the scene, "It is a fine morning." I noticed
there was no trace of the Irish in his speech that I had become used to. He took off his hat and made a small bow.
"I fear I have caused this gentleman some inconvenience.
He is of your party?" He managed to sound astonished.

Mr. Edward obviously found it difficult to admit such a
thing and merely said, "We make our way to the meet,
sir."

"Ah," said Captain Jack, "how I wish I could join you,
but"—here he patted his throat, covered nearly to his ears
on this day by a cream-colored stock instead of a green
one—"I am here for my health. Your high places help my
lungs." Then he drew himself very upright in his saddle,
like a sick man forcing himself, and said, "Captain Egerton, sir, of the—" and he named a regiment.

Mr. Edward now introduced himself, staring a little, as
though something about the stranger puzzled him, and
presented Sir William Wynne.

At the last name Captain Jack bowed again. "I have
heard of you, sir. And this gentleman?" indicating with a
turn of his head the strangely silent Gowan.

"Captain Hunter Gowan, sir," said Mr. Edward. "And
now . . ."

"Of course, I must detain you no further. I apologize for my absent-mindedness. I was admiring your vista," he said, and began to rein his horse to the side. Then he paused and said, "Hunter Gowan? Not the thief-taker from the hills of Wicklow?"

"The magistrate, sir!" roared Gowan.

"And where the deuce did you acquire the rank of captain?" The disdain in his voice was entirely insulting.

"From Sir William Wynne, damn your insolence and will you GET OUT OF MY WAY!"

Here Captain Jack pulled his horse across the road again. "I have heard of you too, sir. This man was in jail" —he addressed Mr. Edward—"for many cruelties committed in Ireland, and was kept there by the English officer commanding. He was released at the instance of those who are now themselves under suspicion. I am compelled to call your companion a murderer! There, sir!" And Captain Jack, apparently much moved, was taken by a fit of coughing that turned him first red and then pale and I greatly wondered at this for he had shown no sign of such feebleness at our last meeting.

Hunter Gowan stood in his stirrups and made a slash at him with his whip which Captain Jack took on his arm, saying quickly, "I shall give you satisfaction. Though I am a sick man." Captain Jack gave us all a wan smile and appeared to stifle a further fit of coughing. "I apologize, gentlemen, for this unpleasantness. The encounter was unexpected and has much moved me. I shall await this gentleman's pleasure. I am at Mrs. Groves's lodgings in the town. I shall be there all this evening. Tomorrow morning would suit me perfectly." Then, brushing past Hunter Gowan who seemed immobilized by fury, he picked his way between us, bowing to Mr. Edward and Sir William, smiling, making polite remarks about the inconvenience he was causing, and continued on his way slowly along the lane.

All of us sat there without moving for a few instants, Gowan slumped in his saddle, saying, "I'll kill him! Kill him! Who is he? Where did he come from?"

I saw Sir William glance at Mr. Edward. "Lodgin's at Mrs. Groves's?" he said. Mr. Edward seemed to understand his question and answered, "An excellent address." Sir William nodded and was, surprisingly, the first of us to move. Turning his horse, he followed Captain Jack at a dignified pace but soon caught up with him. It was not possible to hear what passed between them but hats were raised, bows exchanged and Sir William turned again and rejoined us, Captain Jack riding slowly on.

"Told him we'd wait on him," he said. "This evenin'. Asked him a question or two. Mutual acquaintances, that sort of thing. Seems a gentleman. All lies of course about Ireland. Of course."

"We shall be late," said Mr. Edward, spurring his horse. "You will be good enough to follow, Gowan. I shall lead." It was the first time I had heard Mr. Edward address him without his rank. "I also am a magistrate. I cannot permit dueling. Besides, he is a sick man."

"Sick or not I'll fight him," said Hunter Gowan.

Mr. Edward gave him a quick glance and to my astonishment said, "Fight if you must," pushed his horse into a canter and we followed.

Behind me I heard Sir William murmur, as though to himself, "Hadn't heard his name, Egerton. Odd that." When I turned round he returned my look with such bland complacence and kept his small blue eyes so unwaveringly on mine that it was I who looked away first. For some reason the steadiness of that gaze of Sir William's gave me more fear, for myself as well as for Captain Jack, than I had known before.

12

The Hunt

The sad thing about the rest of the day was that it was filled with excellent sport, but my head was so full of this other matter I could hardly enjoy it. We drew five coverts, and each of them gave us a chase across open country in fine weather which would have raised the whole hunt's spirits, were it not for the behavior of Hunter Gowan. He was now quite mad, it seemed to me, cursing and whooping and roaring, driving his horse into a lather. This would not have been so bad, for people often grew heated in the sport, but he sometimes overran the hounds causing great confusion and annoyance, so that Mr. Edward was at a loss to explain his companion to the rest of the county. But this was not all: there was something worse, and without it my belief is that he would have been ordered home by the Master. What this other thing was is difficult to describe, but if you take into account the fine day, the fine sport, the beauty of the country we rode over, and if I say that because of Gowan there was something horrible among these things, something cruel, devilish, insane, as though a new element had been introduced, a sense of horror, you may have some hint of what I mean. He was a smallish man, and in terms of the great folk there, quite insignificant, but they drew away from him as though afraid of the air that surrounded him.

The prospect of fighting a sick man had clearly raised his spirits past the point of frenzy; and I guessed, or at least I hoped, that Captain Jack had been feigning illness in order to bring about just this eagerness. For, Hunter Gowan being a bully, I presumed he would be a coward. I had to admit he showed no fear; quite the contrary. He took ditches and walls in his stride, with a boldness unjustified in so poor a horseman. He also took many tumbles, until he was coated with mud, but always caught his horse and mounted again as though nothing had happened.

At the last kill he exceeded himself, even usurping the job of the Duke's Huntsman. The fox had gone to ground near some buildings, and, dismounting, Hunter Gowan pursued the hounds on foot before the Huntsman could stop him. It turned out that the fox was hidden in a cesspit belonging to a farmhouse, and had got into it through some broken brickwork. It had breathed its last among the filth, and Hunter Gowan, on his knees, stuck his head and shoulders inside and emerged with the dead fox, shouting with triumph. Then he cut off the beast's

stinking brush and stuck it in his hat! Returning to the
rest of the astonished hunt, he offered the brush to one or
two of the ladies who were with us and they refused the
object with horror, covered as it was with ordure—as indeed was Hunter Gowan. Then, breaking every rule, for
it was not his place to do so, he hurled the body of the fox
to the hounds, screaming over and over, "Tear him in
pieces! Tear him in pieces!"

This, or something like it, is the custom at the kill, but
never before had I seen it done with such craziness, or by
anyone other than the Huntsman.

I saw the Duke draw Mr. Edward aside, with glances
in the direction of the blood-daubed stinking Captain,
and I saw Mr. Edward frown and begin to talk very rap-
idly. He was doubtless absolving himself of responsibility
for his guest, for then the Duke spoke to Sir William
Wynne, of whose ho's and hum's he had to make the
best sense he could. At all events Sir William left him,
with a deep obeisance, and rejoined us for our homeward
ride looking not in the least put out.

Mr. Edward's thoughts, once he had mastered his anger
at the shame brought upon him by the behavior of
Gowan, turned to the subject of the duel. He seemed almost eager for it to take place, and I suspected this was
because he had seen in the duel, whatever its outcome, a
way of at last ridding himself of Hunter Gowan.

Many difficulties remained, however, and these he
discussed with Sir William, who had no fears about the
success of his favorite. "First-rate shot, sir," he assured
Mr. Edward. "First-rate. Settle that feller."

"I am in a difficult position, Sir William. As a magistrate . . . and yet, such an insult . . ."

"Know a place? Secret. No one about?"

"That *could* be found . . ." said Mr. Edward, thinking. "There is a disused quarry, not my own, not anyone's. The ownership has been in dispute for many years . . ."

"You'll be present?" said Sir William.

"I think so, yes," said Mr. Edward, to my surprise. But when I looked at his set face, it crossed my mind that detesting law-breaking as he did he nevertheless intended to give his countenance to this fight, to make sure it was indeed a duel and not a murder. He went on, "I will be open with you, Sir William. I will permit this duel to take place—in view of the appalling insult put upon the Adjutant of my kinsman—on condition of perfect secrecy."

"Of course," said Sir William.

"And on condition, should the affair end fatally—to either party—that you will convey the . . . body . . . with you into Wales."

Sir William considered this, looking at Mr. Edward with that same air of amiable blandness he had turned upon me, but his mind was clearly turning over the dangers of this course. At last he said, "Can be done. Casualty of war. In a way. Agreed."

Hunter Gowan took no part in this conversation, for in contrast to his behavior when we set out, he now trailed behind, a filthy and morose figure; as though, and it was hardly surprising, his flow of animal spirits had at last failed him.

We boys kept as near the two gentlemen as we dared, hardly breathing in case we missed anything of their conference, and although we said nothing I was quite certain that each of us had privately sworn that no power on earth would keep him from being present at this duel. Mr. Turner was with us, though why he came we could not understand. He took no part in the hunt. Now he tried to distract us from our eavesdropping with a discourse about hunting scenes in Ovid, but we paid him no attention and Mr. Edward gave him a look of such impatience that in the end he desisted, and we rode on in silence, tired, each busy with his own thoughts.

At last Sir William spoke, and again it was as though to himself. "I wonder if that feller . . ." and he stopped.

"Yes?" said Mr. Edward.

"There's a runaway captain we're after. Gowan says they had trouble with him in Wexford. This one knew something of Gowan, didn't he? Amusin' if it were he, puttin' his head in the noose. They often do."

"Who?"

"Criminals. Wait, and they come."

"He did not look like a criminal," said Mr. Edward.

"How should a criminal look?" said Sir William innocently. "General Hunter . . . the Officer Commanding he spoke of. Hunter came from England, thought he knew the country. Didn't. We had rebels bottled up with their families. Place called Macamores. Got permission to finish the lot off. Hunter stopped us. Sent a Brigadier chap called Fitzgerald—damned Papist—to talk with 'em. Comes back, says not rebels, just hungry. Gowan tells Hunter, 'Protestants massacred if we don't kill this crowd.' Hunter laughs, calls him 'Mr. Massacre.' Claps him in jail by God!"

"And were the Protestants massacred?"

"Would have been. We took measures."

"Despite the Army?"

"Despite some of it. Despite that Hunter chap. Didn't know the country. We had him moved. Influence. Useful."

Mr. Edward stared. "I did not know the Army was

against the Militia and the Militia disobedient to the Army."

"No good, that kind of man," said Sir William genially, "trying to spare 'em. Irish so damned poor, d'you see. Follow anyone. Better dead. Safer." That seemed to conclude Sir William's thoughts on the matter; and these, for him, had been surprisingly long speeches. We continued the rest of the way, as before, in silence: Hunter Gowan—Mr. Massacre—taking up the rear.

When we arrived back at the manor it was nearly dark, and I was invited in with the rest. We were served warmed wine in front of the hall fire, and I had to admit that, in spite of the wine and the fire, this was always a less cheerful occasion at the manor than it was at other houses I had visited. There was something about Mr. Edward, he unbent so little, that cast a chill, though I had never seen him discourteous to anyone except Hunter Gowan. Today of course he was more than usually preoccupied, and it seemed to me again that his apparent eagerness for the duel masked a by now desperate desire to be rid of his two guests. Almost at once he dismissed the servants and ordered that our little group be left alone. Speaking quietly, he revealed that the problem which now concerned him was how to get news of the arrangements to Captain Egerton. Always, that is, supposing that he was not willing to withdraw his insult and apologize. For if a duel was to take place next morning, the details must be given him tonight.

Sir William was obviously too great a personage to be made a messenger, and Mr. Edward would not, despite their entreaties, use his sons. His eye fell upon Mr. Turner, who turned pale, but I was watching Mr. Edward closely for reasons of my own, and I saw he dismissed Mr. Turner from his thoughts before the evidence of his fright became clear. That left me; and Mr. Edward stared anxiously, at last, in my direction.

"Francis," he said. "You are tired, as we all are, but will you do it? I shall explain matters to your mother. Indeed," he said, "it is the need to involve you in this miserable business that weighs on me most heavily. I fear your mother will never forgive me. But what alternative is there? I dare not involve anyone in the village, nor any of the servants—and, gentlemen, boys, I must command you that not one word of this ever goes outside this room—so there remains only you. Would you take Nimrod and ride to Cheltenham, attend upon Captain Egerton with Captain Hunter Gowan's compliments, and if he will not withdraw in writing, inform him of the arrangements I shall describe to you?"

The thought of riding Nimrod, the best horse in Mr. Edward's stable, would have been enough to make me forget any tiredness that I felt. But of all the commissions I could have been given, this was the one I most desired. Now, at last, I was to be fully involved with Scarf Jack again: I should witness all, be a part of all and in a position to give him all the help that I could.

Of course I agreed at once, to the jealousy of my cousins, and quickly Mr. Edward gave me my instructions, as though by haste he would the sooner have the whole business behind him.

"You know Elwes' Quarry? You will ask Captain Egerton if he wishes to withdraw his offensive words, and if he chooses not to do so you must tell him that Captain Hunter Gowan desires him to be at that place just before first light tomorrow. The fight will be with pistols, one shot apiece, at forty paces."

"At ten!" said Hunter Gowan, who had been muttering to himself while Mr. Edward was talking, as though drunk.

"That would be murder, sir," said Mr. Edward quietly, and continued, "At forty paces, and a wounding to be considered satisfaction enough."

"No!" roared Gowan.

"I would remind you that I am empowered to detain you on suspicion of a duel," said Mr. Edward, "to arrest you immediately after the duel, and commit you to jail. This I shall not hesitate to do if you do not obey. It will not be your first experience of confinement, I understand."

Gowan started from his place, and only a series of ho's and hum's from Sir William prevented him from making for Mr. Edward, who took no notice of him at all. "A wounded man, if capable, is to remove himself from the scene immediately. We are not able to provide a medical attendant, but Captain Egerton may bring one if he is able to do so. Do you understand all that?"

I said that I did and made to leave. Mr. Edward detained me. "You cannot return tonight. I cannot have you making that journey back, so late. Here is some money for your lodging," and he gave me a guinea. "Here also," he said, going to a case that lay on the hall table, "is a pistol, which I believe you know how to use." He smiled as he said this, because our forbidden practice with this pistol had, last year, earned my cousins and myself a beating. "I must be able to assure your mother that all possible measures for your safety have been taken. I have no fears for you"—he put his hand on my arm uncertainly, unused to making such gestures—"and you must have no fears for your mother left unattended. I shall call at your house myself, within the hour, and bring her here. She will need the comfort of Mrs. Edward until your safe return. At the quarry, then, at dawn."

Sir William Wynne was yawning and stretching by now, as though all this were the most ordinary business in the world; Hunter Gowan was emptying his tankard and refilling it from the jug, as though this was the last wine in the house and he was determined to have it all; as for my cousins, they could not disguise their sulky looks as I marched out of the hall to go and saddle up Nimrod.

13

Cornelius Grogan

He was impatient in his stall, for his stablemates had been out all day and he resented being left behind. But Mr. Edward rarely used him for hunting, being more than usually fond of him and fearful that he might be injured. I reckoned that with Nimrod's help I could be in the town within the hour, or just about, and so miss the worst of the footpads if there were any. These usually waited until later, for revelers returning home with fuddled wits, and the watchmen dozing. The charged pistol in my pocket gave me comfort, so did the well-stowed guinea, and it was in high spirits that I rode out of the stable into the dark.

A frost had fallen, the sky was clear, and with Orion bright at my back I set our faces towards Cheltenham, on the road I had gone with Joel. The frost had already made the going firmer, the ruts which had caused Joel some trouble were now harder, and though Nimrod slipped sometimes on the descent, he was sure-footed and strong and soon I was glad to be safely within the lights of Gallows Oak Pike.

I paid my due, the lodgekeeper grumbling at having to give me money for a guinea, and I was told that Mrs. Groves's lodging house was within a few minutes' ride. It was easy to find from his description: a fine new house standing a little apart from others with an entrance for horses and carriages at the side. I rode straight in and was met by an ostler, to whom I gave a shilling for him to find fresh straw and a drink for Nimrod. Feeling rather grand, and thinking I might as well get my shilling's worth, I dismounted and threw the reins to him and asked for stabling for the night. Perhaps Captain Jack might be able to find me a bed, but even if he could not I had seen at once that no horse was likely to find better-kept lodgings than these.

I went back through the courtyard to the front of the house and rang the bell. One half of the large door was opened by a girl servant to whom I gave my name. She politely asked me inside, and I waited in the hall while she climbed the stairs to announce me. For once in my life I did not feel out of place in such a hall, I suppose because I had reason to be there. But also, I think, because I knew Captain Jack was at hand, and although there were things about him which frightened me a little, I felt I could trust him to put me at my ease. I was soon proved right, because there was the noise of quick steps on the landing and a cry, "Francis! Well met! Come up, come up!" and as I approached the stairs I saw Captain Jack bending over the banisters and looking down with a great smile on his face. I passed the girl coming down and she was smiling also, as though the new guest was already a favorite.

After grasping my hand and pumping it, saying, "Good to see you, Francis! Good to see you! How was your day? Was the good Hunter Gowan in form? I'd have left Ireland just to see the look on his face this morning!" and roaring with laughter (there was no need for me to ask whether the illness of the morning had been feigned), he drew me between two high doors which stood open, into a room that was even higher, with wonderful plaster patterns on the ceiling, and with further double doors at the end wall which I supposed led to other rooms.

It was a grand apartment, even finer than the oak-paneled drawing room at the manor which up to this time was the most splendid private room I had seen. The furnishings and hangings were rich and the room was lit by four chandeliers with many fresh candles on them.

After my quick climb up the stairs I was a little breathless and perhaps dazed, for when, with Captain Jack's hand on my shoulder, I heard a pleasant, drawling voice with a touch of Irish in it say, "So this is the boy is it, Jack?" I could not at first see where the voice came from.

"It is indeed," said Captain Jack, "Master Francis Place. This is Major Grogan, Francis: Cornelius Grogan, an old comrade and an old friend."

Sprawled untidily in a winged armchair that was turned towards the fire, so that he was nearly hidden from view, was a pale delicate-looking man with thin brown hair, and with one leg stuck stiffly out in front of him. From the depths of his chair he levered himself up with some difficulty, and held out his hand to me, smiling. He was in shirt and breeches, like Captain Jack, and had still gray eyes and a gentle manner. "That was a good turn you did last Wednesday night," he said. "I knew Jack had nine lives, but I think he would have used the last of them but for you. Come in and sit down. Have you had supper? No matter if you have, you shall sup again. So shall we, Jack. All this claret . . ." and he limped to the bell rope and gave it a pull.

I now saw there were empty wine bottles and dirty glasses everywhere, and guns and fishing rods and whips, and muddy boots thrown in a corner under a statue of a naked lady, and altogether the sort of disorder, in that stately apartment, that my mother would not have allowed for a moment, and which made me feel at home at once. I took the chair he offered me, he sank back into his own, and Captain Jack threw himself into another and then sat forward quickly, slapping his knees with delight. "It's good to see you again! What with jawing over old times with Con, I had almost forgot my friends at Elstone. My faith, but it's a windy spot you have up there, and a lonely one, but good for our purpose, eh? What news have you brought us? But shush!"

The maid had knocked at the door in answer to Major Grogan's summons. He ordered a fine supper of neck of mutton, cold tongue, small beer; then, with a glance at me and a smile, some ice cream. He asked for more claret, this time looking at Captain Jack. "Three bottles?"

"If we're to talk all night! Why not? You're the finest host in England, Con; it's lucky you're now so rich or you'd soon see the bottom of your pocket."

"I don't remember you ever stinting me, Jack. Oh, and

some brandy. A bottle." The maidservant seemed very amused by all this and withdrew, blushing a little.

"You're very well fixed here, Con," said Captain Jack, staring thoughtfully after the maid, who was very pretty. "Good as Dublin."

The Major turned to the fire. "Dublin was no place to be with that sort of news coming in, the same cruelties to our poor people over and over and me no use to man nor beast. I might have known you'd be mixed up in it, though." He turned to Captain Jack, but receiving no response from the other man, who merely bent his head and looked at his hands, Major Grogan sank back again into his chair as though tired, and said, "So, not fancying London for the same reason I didn't fancy Dublin, I thought I'd try the country." Here he smiled at me. "But I've been damned dull, Jack, till we met."

"Do you know how I ran into him?" said Jack, amazed. "Not as Hunter Gowan nearly ran into me! God, I thought he'd have me over. What a sack of potatoes that man is on a horse! No; as soon as you'd got the money to me—for which a thousand thanks!—I got myself down here and who did I meet at the tailors, getting himself fitted out, too, but the one man in the world I would have wished? Isn't that a fine chance? 'Jack's luck,' eh, Con? D'you remember?"

"I do," said the other, gravely. "That was a good time ago, do *you* remember? We were younger then."

"And d'you know, he can patch me up too, if Gowan's finger does not shake so much he can't pull the trigger? Con's a sawbones. I beg his pardon—a Surgeon Major."

The Major laughed a little sadly. "Now I talk ladies out of headaches brought on by too much cardplaying, and try to convince them the waters will cure them. At least, here I do. Though I sipped the waters once myself and how they manage to stomach the stuff I can't imagine. But Jack—all that soldiering *was* a long time ago for me. Are you sure this desperate business at home hasn't turned your head?"

"Of course it has!" said Jack, laughing. "It would turn yours too."

"A man's judgment is all at odds after a battle," said Major Grogan. "He's overexcited. D'you remember in America, how many of us came through safely, and then got hurt in the next one as though some damned madness had got into us, or we were disgusted with ourselves for being still alive?"

"I *am* a bit mad, Con," said Jack, seriously. "No, I know you didn't say that, but you meant it. The job in Ireland was so crazy—and useful—I screwed myself up to it so tight I doubt if I'll ever unscrew again. I was frightened the whole time. Never think soldiers aren't frightened," he said to me. "Wounds hurt. Ask Con. They can ruin a man's life, they can take his life away forever. For no good reason usually. A soldier's life is stupefying. You get so used to pain and death in others, you hardly notice until it happens to you. If you survive you're half-mad, and half-wanting to die yourself. It's strange, but that's what happens. You ought to know about it. I won't have you going for a soldier."

"That's good fatherly advice you're being given, Francis," said Major Grogan, smiling at Captain Jack; and I remembered him holding his hand out over the river and saying it was black with blood. Despite the fire, I felt cold. It was true that since Captain Jack had arrived in our neighborhood there had been, underneath the excitement, a kind of horror in the air. And there was more to come.

"This Hunter Gowan business, Jack. That's madness too. If he finds out who you are, he'll shoot you like a dog. So will Wynne and his cutthroats."

"Listen, Con. You say you've changed. But you still think I'm the young idiot you knew. Perhaps I behave like it sometimes. But I'm not a boy any more. I've had time to do plenty of thinking up in Francis's village. Up there I could have come from behind a tree and slit Gowan's throat twenty times over, and revenged the murders of old men, of babies—I've seen this, Con—and have prevented him from doing more. I dreamed of this, sweated over it, I could have done it and been gone. But no, at last I said to myself 'No!' And you know why? Because I felt something terrible coming up inside me. You know what it was? Justified hatred! A hatred and an instinct for murder, that felt itself completely justified. That's devil's work! Only God himself can feel as justified as that. Then, when I shared this murderous feeling that Gowan himself must live with, then did I feel myself mad, poisoned, ruined: no different at all from that devil. So I said no! and I thank God I was given the strength and the grace to say no. You think it is crazy to face him in the open and so it is, but it's the first sane thing I've done for months. It makes me human again, not some damned soul, some butcher who thinks he's God, like—Hunter Gowan!"

The Major was silent for a space. Then he smiled. "You're a case all right, Jack. Perhaps I should prescribe you a dose of the Cheltenham waters . . . Look at the boy, we've his eyes popping out of his head. Ah, here comes the food."

The maid came in with a tray, and soon I was eating a supper as fine as any I have tasted since; and it was my first taste of ice cream. Captain Jack took a spoonful too. As we ate the men talked, the Major smiling at Jack's memories and stories, but saying little himself. Though when he did speak it was always to return to the exact nature of Jack's involvement in Ireland. It was clear that this worried him, and it was equally clear that Captain Jack was not being entirely frank. I felt that Major Grogan hoped he might be more forthcoming in front of me.

"You were on the side of the rebels?"

"I was."

"With Brigadier Fitzgerald's connivance?"

"He knew I was there, certainly. We shared the view that if the militia and the yeomanry were to have their heads and all their bloody acts be blamed on the Army, Ireland might not be wholly pacified for a hundred years."

"Jack, did you fire on the King's troops?"

"I did not."

"But you caused others to do so?"

"For God's sake, Con, those rebels were as loyal to the Crown as you and I—if they knew what the Crown was. They were driven past endurance by Hawtry White, Archie Jacob, Hunter Gowan and the rest of the crew you hate as much as I do. They were being killed, their houses burned, no one pausing to ask if they were loyal to the Crown or not. It may be an odd sort of loyalty *I* have, but I felt that as a British soldier—for at least I had been one, and as a Catholic, by choice too—I owed it to them *and* to the honor of the Army, to help them. All I know how to use is a sword, and why should I use it only on the winning side?"

"We were not always on the winning side, Jack."

"No, and there were things about our fight in America that turned your stomach too, or do you not remember?"

"I do," said Major Grogan, with a touch of coolness.

"Because you sympathized with the rebels! There, you see?" Jack was triumphant.

"But sympathy is one thing, and—oh . . ." He gave up and changed his direction. "You never told me you were a Catholic!"

"It was after I left the Service. It seemed honest, feeling for the Catholics as I do. Besides," he laughed, "you know I love authority."

Major Grogan laughed also. "I had not noticed. But was your father not a clergyman?"

"I waited till he had gone. I saw no need to distress him. But—look!" Waving his fork he returned to the attack. "Your brother is a good landlord. Both you and he have spoken up about the condition of the peasants under bad ones, and under these present laws. What more did I do but try and make happen what you know *should* happen?"

"But legality, Jack. The *law*, for goodness' sake!"

"And when the law has broken down? When mad dogs like Gowan are turned loose? . . . You see? It's not so easy, Con."

"Well, let's leave it for now. The boy's dead beat. What about tomorrow then? I'll be breaking the law tomorrow it seems," he turned to me, "if Jack has his way."

"God, I nearly forgot! Francis, how can you forgive me . . . What about tomorrow, then? Are we to fight?"

I did not make the formal request for an apology because I knew that would be a waste of time, so I told him the arrangements Mr. Edward had decided upon and both men nodded. Major Grogan said, "That's an early

start and you must get some sleep, boy. You've had a
day's hunting. I've an old campaign bed. Shall I put it up
for you in a corner? Then Jack and I can crack on and
you can get some rest."

I was more than delighted to stay with these two old
soldiers, so Major Grogan limped to the inner room which
I supposed was his bedroom, and came back with a pair
of blankets and what looked like an oblong box of canvas,
with wooden crosspieces. These were like the letter x and
he pulled them till they opened and tautened the canvas
above them, and the box was stretched into a fine bed.
This he put in a corner for me, handing me the blankets
and telling where the privy was on the landing, which I
had been concerned to know for some little while. When
I came back into the room he and Jack were again
stretched in their chairs, glasses in hand, and looked a
most comfortable pair.

So, taking off my coat and boots, feeling an old cam-
paigner already in my soldier's bed with my two com-
rades near at hand, I pretended to compose myself for
sleep, for I wished to hear more of their conversation. But
I must have been more tired than I knew, because it was
a struggle to stay awake. I heard Major Grogan ask where
Captain Jack would go when he had finished his business
here and Jack told him America—or France.

"France!" said Major Grogan, startled. "Our enemy?"

"Maybe it's the only chance for Ireland, help from
there. I tell you I don't know! The situation was changing
by the day. Leave it! If I'm ever a traitor then you can
hang me. But I swear to God I don't think I've been one
yet."

Major Grogan's reply I could not hear. I thought,
though, that he understood Captain Jack's position better

than I did, and it occurred to me that perhaps words like "traitor" and "loyal" were not always as easy to understand as I had imagined. I heard the sound of glasses being filled and Captain Jack say, "Talking of turning coats . . . d'you fancy a ride tomorrow? If I settle Gowan the rest'll be after me. Will you change coats with me and lead 'em a chase?"

For the first time that night I heard Major Grogan laugh aloud. "Now *that* I like the sound of! God, Jack, no wonder you've lasted so long!"

Then steps came towards my bed in the corner and Captain Jack stood over me, rearranging my coat which I had spread over the top of the blankets. Feeling it heavy he reached into the pocket and took out the pistol. Then he looked towards me and seeing my eyes open said, "D'you know how to use this?"

"I think so, sir."

"I could wish you did not," he said. He stared down at me for a moment. "Did you hear any talk of Gowan's skill with a pistol?"

I thought that he was at last afraid and I did not know how to answer him. He persisted. "Did you?"

"I—heard Sir William Wynne say that he was a perfect shot, sir."

Jack gave a great shout of delighted laughter. "Did you, by God! I'm delighted to hear he's perfect in some way. D'you hear that, Con? Gowan can shoot straight!"

"Let's hope so, Jack, for your sake," said Major Grogan.

This was too great a mystery for me. All I knew was that my friends must have some kind of scheme. I stared up at Captain Jack as once he had stared up at me. To my surprise he bent and kissed me on the forehead. "Good night, Francis," he said. "Fear nothing at all. We'll meet in the morning."

14

The Meeting at Dawn

It seemed not the morning but the middle of the night when Jack awoke me, holding a candle in my face and shaking my shoulder roughly, as though regretting his tenderness of the previous night. "Come on, slug-a-bed! D'ye want to sleep the whole day?"

Whether it was this rough handling that annoyed me or whether I was startled into frankness I don't know, but I found myself saying, "You seem to have two voices."

"How's that?" he said, frowning at me.

"You did not speak in that Irish way to Mr. Edward."

"Because he's an English gentleman and they only understand their own sort of speech. Any other sort belongs

to the barbarians. This makes life easy for them—if a little
restricted. And I'm not the only one! Did I tell you that,
Con?" He called to the next room, the doors of which
stood open. "The night we met this lad pretended to be a
shepherd!" Major Grogan, his face lathered, a towel about
his neck, put his head round the door. "You two have
much in common," he said, and disappeared back to his
shaving.

Jack seemed in great spirits, quite dressed except for
his coat, the green scarf about his neck and munching a
hunk of bread he tore from the loaf we had for supper.
Then he put his head over a basin and poured a jug of
water over it, rubbing the water into the back of his neck
and into his short-cropped hair. He spluttered and gasped
and toweled himself vigorously, announcing that he had
never felt better in his life.

As I pulled on my boots Grogan came into the room
adjusting his neckcloth. He was in a straw-colored suit
with breeches and stockings of a color nearly the same
and he looked very dignified. He went to a table and
opened a small case. Inside it was a pair of pistols and as
he turned them over, so did my stomach turn, at this re-
minder of our business. Then his eyes sought those of
Captain Jack and he waited until they were met by
the eyes of his friend before he spoke. "Do you want to go
on with this?" he said. "There would be no dishonor at all
if you mounted your horse and rode away."

"The waiting's bad, Con." Captain Jack shook his head
and sighed, rubbing his hand over his dampened hair.
"All this fussing with courtesies . . . Do *you* want to go
on with it? It's you I've dragged in."

"Well," said Grogan, carefully cutting himself a piece
from the loaf, "I shall either be present at the death of

Hunter Gowan—which no man can regret—or the death of you, Jack, which I cannot enjoy. As well as that, unless we're damned lucky and news of this business does not leak out, I shall have to quit this place and I shall miss my comforts. If we're unluckier still I shall miss you. No, I don't look forward to it. I don't even agree with it. But we've known each other a long time, Jack. Maybe my life's become *too* comfortable."

Jack laughed and turned to me. "You wouldn't like to fight for me, would you?" He laughed again when he saw my face and moved quickly to the table. "Here. A minute," and he paused to fill a small flask from the remains of the brandy that stood on the table. This he placed carefully in the pocket of his coat, which lay on a chair. Then, with difficulty, for his coat now seemed too heavy for him, he struggled his arms into its sleeves, smiling at Grogan. "Well—there it is," he said, reaching for his hat and stepping to the door. There he turned and took a long look round the room, Major Grogan standing aside. Grogan bowed very slightly, and Captain Jack looked at him for an instant. Then he clapped his tall hat on his head, strode first through the doorway, and ran down the stairs with us behind him.

In the stables we saddled our horses by lantern light and I could not help remarking on the splendor of my friends' mounts, which were even finer than Nimrod. Their gear, too, was of the very best, the saddles of the new kind that fitted closely to the horse's back without a pommel, which are so good for fast riding and for jumping. Seeing my admiration, Jack patted his horse's neck. "Like him? We have to thank you, and the cross."

I turned away to tighten the girth under Nimrod's

belly, which made it easier for me to ask again, "Why did they not take it from you?"

"The Irish poor have not learned to rob."

"But they can kill."

"They have good teachers," he said coldly, swinging himself up into his saddle and riding a few paces out of the stable, displeased. He took a turn in the courtyard but he had not finished with me. He came back to me as I mounted and said, "On the bridge at Wexford the Catholics killed some Protestant gentlemen who were prisoners. They should not have done that. But the men they murdered had their pockets stuffed with money, for they had hoped to escape. They were thrown in the river dead, their pockets untouched. You'll find something fine in that one day. Yes, they can kill," and he rode ahead once more.

Major Grogan and I were left together in silence. It was cold and still dark; a damp, silent, miserable sort of darkness. Before we reached the turnpike, Captain Jack rode back to us and asked me to lead us round the back of it in case anyone was stirring there. This I did, uncertainly, for I was not sure of another way, but I could just see the dark mass of Leckhampton Hill above us, and as long as that was before me I could not go far wrong. A dog barked at Southfield Farm as we skirted round it but we regained the track where it began to climb without being disturbed, and the only sound before we reached it was the sound of our bridles and the sucking noise of our hooves in the wet turf.

It took us perhaps half an hour to climb to the top and then we continued on the flat for a while before we reached the last hill.

"You live on top of a mountain, Francis," said Jack on

one of his brief visits back to us. He seemed to want to work up in himself a kind of energy and the way he rode back and forth reminded me of Hunter Gowan on the morning of the hunt. I told him we were proud of being hill people and not like the soft people who lived on the plain, and Jack called back quietly, "D'you hear that, Con, you dwell in the plains of Sodom and Gomorrah!"

"Not much longer do I," came the mournful reply from the darkness behind, and Jack laughed. Now that he recognized the way he grew even more impatient and I had Major Grogan for sole companion again.

"This is no place for a boy, Francis," he said softly. "If I told you to be off home, would you go? No," he answered himself. "But it's a trap we're going into. There may be more shooting than even Jack would wish for. Whatever it is he does wish for . . . You stay by the horses, and if shooting starts hold them and get behind them. Do you understand that?"

"I do, sir."

"I wish I knew whether Captain Place had put himself beyond the law or not. I've never really known." I heard him chuckle in the darkness. "The man he's facing is not outside the law it seems, but he should be."

"Sir?"

"Yes, Francis?"

"You called him Captain Place. That's my name."

"Mm? Oh, there may well be a reason, there may not be. He's as many names as I have shirts and needs them all. It seems there isn't a party in the world that wouldn't hang him. He tries to *help* people. Ach! I'm better off with my fishing rod at Framilode . . . We'll do our best to pull him out of this one though, won't we, Francis?"

"Oh yes," I said.

"That's as it should be." I could hear his saddle creak as he turned to look at me in the dark. "Well said. Now hold those horses when the time comes. Don't let them go for an instant. We may need them."

At last we reached the outskirts of our village and after a moment's hesitation I indicated the track that led to the quarry. This doubt on my part gave rise to a cruel impatience in Captain Jack and I saw how he could be a Tartar to those below him. While I was thinking he began tapping his thigh with his whip and at last he demanded to be informed whether I knew the way or whether I did not. The truth was that I had always approached the quarry, which lay about a mile and a half from our village, from across the fields and never from this direction. At the next turning I again hesitated, everything looked different in the half-light, and fear of Captain Jack made me flustered so I decided, blindly, that this *must* be the way and to my great relief it was. I stopped us by the high and tangled brambles that grew over the entrance to it, with a gap between them just wide enough for a cart to pass through.

Captain Jack wasted no time thanking me but said, "I'll go in first. You never know with this kind of fowl."

"I'll not argue," said Major Grogan.

Captain Jack cautiously guided his horse between the high bushes and was gone for only a short while before he reappeared, waving for us to follow. "They're there all right, and not too many. Wynne may have made a gentleman out of Gowan but I doubt it! What a place, Francis. It stinks!"

It did stink a little, of rotting harness, old mattresses, boots, rats. It was the dumping ground for the village and when I was younger many of my treasures had been found here, a broken cartwheel, a stag's horn that must have been kept for a while by someone and then thrown away, a pair of rusted one-handed sheep shears and many other things that I carried home with my friends to my mother's despair.

"And what a place to die," I heard Major Grogan mutter to himself and I suppose it was disgusting, at least to begin with, because most of the dumping was done near the entrance. Once you were past that you were in an open space, not quarried very deep but not to be seen from the road. Small ash trees had rooted themselves at the sides below the rock walls, and elders and thorns, but the center was clear. At the far end was a gentle slope that led to taller trees with an open ride between them which was the way the stones had been taken from the quarry to the village. It was in front of this ride, and raised a little above us, that the other party had ranged themselves; or were just doing so, for they had arrived at about the same time and had come the way I knew, across the fields.

"Good morning, gentlemen," called Captain Jack, his voice echoing from the walls of stone, and from the figures at the far end of the quarry there came no reply. There was Hunter Gowan himself, on horseback, next to him Sir William Wynne who even in the small light that was now growing appeared to be as colorfully clad as always, and on a little eminence overlooking the scene I could just make out Mr. Edward and his sons. I was not surprised to see my cousins there because I knew that short of locking them up Mr. Edward could find no way to prevent them from attending.

Major Grogan nosed his horse slowly forward from our group and as he did so Sir William began towards him at the same pace. So they approached, each man moving as the other did, and as a result of this, when they met, it was precisely in the center of the space as though it were a parade ground and they were executing a piece of drill. Their horses faced each other nose to nose, while the two riders conferred. Then each turned and rode as slowly back.

"By God, Con, you have the air of a man who's done all this before!"

"I've seen it done."

"Beautiful! You're a credit to me. Now would you mind telling me what passed between you and that Montgolfier balloon on horseback?"

"I asked Sir William what would satisfy his principal and he said a full denial of the words you put upon him and a public apology before all these present."

"And you said?"

Major Grogan ignored this interruption, obviously determined to observe the formalities. "Sir William then asked what would satisfy my principal and I said he wished Captain Hunter Gowan to leave Ireland and the people of Ireland, to the endless benefit of both."

"Well said. And?"

"The conditions being unacceptable to both parties it was agreed to fight, with pistols, each party to take twenty paces before firing and I shall call the paces."

"Well, then—"

"When there is a little more light."

"Dammit, I have no gift for waiting!" Jack's horse, as though infected by the impatience of his rider, kept sidestepping and turning. "How long d'you think it will be?"

We all studied the sky. The sun was not yet up on a day that looked as though it had already decided to be gray and overcast. But in the East, to our left, there was a show of increasing brightness and the figures before us were becoming gradually more clear.

"Five minutes," said Grogan. "Perhaps a little more."

"God Almighty! All right." And Captain Jack wheeled his nervous horse and began to pace it up and down the narrow space between the sides of the quarry at our end. Major Grogan sat quite still, composed, almost hostile in his correctness, and the group on the other side were still also, as the increasing light picked out details of their clothes and faces. Captain Jack was the only person moving, and a low laugh, clearly from Gowan, came to us from the other end of the quarry. Captain Jack was still at once, his head jerking round towards his adversary, and this laugh struck me as a piece of good fortune. He badly needed to be made angry. To my mind, and I think to that of Major Grogan, he was taking the matter too lightly. Forty paces for a good shot is not too far and I was visited by a dreadful picture of Captain Jack lying on the ground with Hunter Gowan huzzaing and riding away to breakfast.

The minutes passed, but slowly. The light grew better, but not much. It was a day that was not going to have a real dawn, it would be nearly as dark as this at noon. It was decided to begin. Sir William Wynne and Major Grogan signaled to each other with handkerchiefs.

As soon as he saw this happen the stiffness seemed to go out of Captain Jack and he began smiling again. "Off you go, Con. Give my respects to Sir William. I'll draw aside for a moment." To me he said, "I'll not shake your hand, Francis. I'll be with you again in a few minutes," and he rode a few paces apart to the side of the quarry.

Major Grogan sat upright on his horse staring in front

of him. "My countrymen disgust me," he said. "We go to our deaths smiling. Why do we love death so much? Why do *you* love death, you fool!" He muttered this as though addressing himself, and turning to where Captain Jack sat on his horse with his head bent, he said, "Well may you say your prayers!" Then he suddenly turned sideways to me and said, almost snarling in his sudden passion, "It takes more courage to *live!* Remember that!"

"Can he do it?" I asked him.

"Live? Today?" Major Grogan was cool again. "Possibly."

"But he must be so tired! For days he has been horribly pressed, ill, a fugitive. Is his life always like this?"

"He's a great irregular soldier, Francis. He learnt much from General Washington. He should be a general himself with ribbons on his coat, not stuck with a rat in a stinking quarry at the back end of nowhere. He thinks too much for a soldier. Heigh ho . . . He thought all this through, your father, let's hope he thought it through well!"

I barely remarked what he said, so naturally did he say "your father."

But he saw me looking at him and he said, "Oh yes, Captain Place is your father. You might as well know it since it might be the first and last you see of him. Ach!" Making his little sound of disgust he spurred his horse and cantered forward to meet Sir William.

15

The Duel

I suppose I should have been overwhelmed by this information, but I was not. I had never thought of my father much. It was my mother I lived with and loved and "Father" was only a word. That he should have arrived by chance and so dramatically did not surprise me, nor that it was so clear he would not stay, for how could such a man stay anywhere?

So I cannot say I looked on Scarf Jack with more interest as he sat, watchfully now, under the yellow quarry wall. I was interested enough anyway. He seemed to me the most extraordinary man in the world, and what else should a father be? After all, the death of my father

would mean little to me. But the death of my friend Scarf
Jack, at the hands of such a one as Gowan, was not to be
thought on. I was a boy, caught up in the excitement of
all these great happenings, but I began to have some real
understanding of their horror, of the feeling Major Grogan had shown from the bottom of his soul.

I knew something else, I think, that morning. Caught
up in the excitement I may have been, but though I would
have trusted my life to Captain Jack in any danger, my
everyday living I would have preferred to trust to Major
Grogan . . .

He and Sir William were now conferring in the center
of the quarry. They had dismounted and were examining
pistols. Then Sir William laid his very white handkerchief
on the ground. They remounted and rode back.

"Francis, you are to hold the horses and stay where
you are," said Major Grogan, dismounting again. "Remember what I told you! Jack, we're to walk to the handkerchief together. Here are your pistols. Load one. Keep
your eyes on our friends over there. When they step forward, so do we." He stood formal as ever, facing Captain
Jack who was seeing to his pistol. When he seemed
satisfied with it Major Grogan said, "Good luck." My father grinned at him. "You know, Con, I'm not sure all
this flummery is the best idea I ever had." "I've told the
boy," said Major Grogan. My father turned to look at me
with no decipherable expression. "Here they come," said
Major Grogan.

My father turned back to him. "Shall we go?"

"Surely."

The two men marched forward in step, side by side,
Major Grogan fighting his limp as best he could, and it

stirred my blood to see those friends step out together so close and with so much understanding between them.

The other pair also approached but did not present a similar picture. Their figures were so grotesquely different: the bulk of Sir William in its extraordinary dress covering the ground with such strange, almost female, smoothness on its little feet, and the hunched body of Gowan, his neck sunk in his shoulders as though he could hardly restrain himself from springing forward; planting his feet stiffly on the ground, like a horse reined back from the gallop.

At last the four men arrived at the handkerchief and stopped. Words were exchanged between Sir William and Major Grogan and then they stepped to opposite sides, leaving Scarf Jack and Hunter Gowan alone together, face to face. Then the enemies turned, their backs almost touching. Major Grogan raised his handkerchief and, bringing it smartly down, called "One! Two!" and they began to take their paces away from each other in time to his call. My heart thumped so painfully I could hardly bear to look—"Five! Six!" went the call—but I could not take my eyes away. I had thought of duels as exciting, but this was horrible. "Nine! Ten!" sang out the clear voice of Major Grogan and then, on the count of ten, Scarf Jack still continuing to walk his further ten paces as agreed, Hunter Gowan turned and, sighting along his gun, fired at Captain Jack's back who staggered, pitched forward and lay still.

For a moment nobody moved. Hunter Gowan stood there, a wisp of smoke drifting from the muzzle of his pistol, the quarry walls still echoing with the shot, fainter and fainter. Then I began to run forward.

"Stay where you are!" Major Grogan's call was as sharp

as the pistol shot and I faltered. Then, with a cry of triumph, Hunter Gowan began to run towards the body of
Captain Jack.

He was almost over him when Captain Jack turned on
his back and with a sweep of his legs sent Hunter Gowan
tumbling. After that things happened so fast it is difficult
to recount them in order. I had barely taken in the shock
of seeing that Captain Jack was apparently unharmed by
a bullet that had surely gone straight into his back, when
Hunter Gowan was on his feet and running, bent double,
as though he feared a shot into his own, and my father
was after him, his undischarged pistol in his hand. Gowan
twisted and turned like a hare, I could hear him panting
and then I could see his eyes rolling in his head because,
to my horror, one of his turns had brought him close to
me and the horses. Then he caught his foot in a root and
fell headlong.

With a roar Captain Jack was on him, pinning his arms
with his knees, his pistol against Gowan's temple. Mr. Edward was spurring his horse down the slope crying,
"Stop, sir! Stop!" and Sir William was standing in the center of the quarry apparently too astonished to move.
Major Grogan, on the other hand, was limping slowly, almost carelessly, towards the two men on the ground as
though he had decided to let matters take their course.

Hunter Gowan's eyes, as he looked up at Captain Jack,
I could see only too clearly. They were calm, as his enemy's eyes had been when he thought he was about to be
hanged. But it was a dead, dull calmness, still with hatred
and danger in it. And the Captain appeared to be in a
frenzy, his mouth twisting, his eyes narrowing and then
widening as though he would have them flash fire, but at
last he moved his gun from Gowan's head and made as if

to cast it aside, though he kept it in his hand, muttering, "*This* is not the way! I wouldn't waste powder and shot on you."

Then a movement from the side of the quarry caught my eye and I saw a man on the top of it, only fifty feet away, sighting a rifle towards us. "Look up to the left!" I cried and I was proud afterwards that I had told Captain Jack in what direction he was to beware. For he looked at once, in the right direction, raised his pistol, resting it on his arm, and fired, it seemed all in one movement, and the man on the quarry edge stayed still for a moment, as though astonished, then his rifle fell from his hand into the quarry, making a clatter, and he followed it himself, his body hitting the ground with a dreadful soft thud. Hunter Gowan was on his feet now, about to run again, when Mr. Edward arrived on his horse, very out of breath. "Know, sir," he said to Gowan, "that you are no longer welcome to my house, no longer a guest of mine, and you are to quit this neighborhood at once. Go, sir, it is no use returning to the manor, the door shall be bolted against you. Who that unfortunate wretch is I intend to discover from Sir William when he has recovered from the stupefaction your conduct has caused him. You, sir," he said to Captain Jack, "are to be complimented on your forbearance. I apologize for the conduct of Captain Hunter Gowan since he seems unable to do so himself, and I hope you consider yourself satisfied by his public disgrace."

This speech cost Mr. Edward much, for he was gasping for breath throughout. His condition was not improved by a crashing and calling through the trees and the appearance of two ruffianly looking men whom I recognized at once as members of the hanging party. These now broke from cover and ran, calling, towards Sir William Wynne.

"Come, Con," said Jack, "we must be off, I think." Climbing quickly onto his horse he called out, "My compliments to you, Mr. Edward, and I am glad we now share an opinion of your guest. I hope one day we may talk and that you will listen. Come, Francis."

"Leave the boy!" said Mr. Edward.

"You shall have him back. And you've got your horse back!"

Meanwhile the men had spoken to Sir William who was now waving his arms calling, "Stop him! Stop him!" and moving swiftly back towards his distant horse. Hunter Gowan ran towards him, listened to what he had to say and joined in the cry, running towards his own.

"It's a great sight!" roared Captain Jack from his horse. "We'll give 'em a chase. Come *on*, boy!" and seeing that I stood dazed he stooped and lifted me bodily, with one arm, until I was astride the horse behind him. "Are you set, Con?" "I am, Jack!" and with a great cry the two men, Jack leading, galloped from the quarry, me with my arms round my father's waist and my cheek pressed to his back.

We had a good start and Jack drove his strong horse hard. When we had traveled about a mile he called a halt and in the lee of a hedge he and Major Grogan exchanged coats. While they were doing so they talked quickly.

"You were right about Gowan, Jack. Did it hurt you?"

"It did. I thought he'd wait till ten though, and aim for the heart, he'd have wanted the fight at ten. Look." Jack showed the inside of his coat where, like armor, were the three layers of thick leather I had seen one of the Bawcombes sewing together, the night I visited Caleb's cottage. He had foreseen, or guessed, everything from the beginning . . . In the center of the leather was a bulge and Jack lifted two of the layers to show how only the last one had stopped the bullet, which was still there. He took it out and threw it to Major Grogan. "A present," he said. "I owe you more than that." "There's something for you in the pocket of my coat," said Major Grogan, struggling with difficulty into Jack's armored one. "When I heard your tale I sent round to the shop and luckily it was there. Now I want no thanks, it might cost us our lives with those scallawags after us. Get off now, Jack, and good luck to you!" Captain Jack had put his hand into the pocket of Grogan's coat and was looking down at his jeweled cross.

Major Grogan, transformed into Captain Jack in his coat and hat, now pointed his horse in the direction of the quarry; his plan, I guessed, being to let the pursuers catch a sight of him and then ride them across country. "I'll have Gowan up to his ears in mud, Jack, never fear," he said, before Captain Jack could thank him for the cross. "I look forward to this. I'll see you again. You'll never die, Jack!" And he was gone. "Don't say that!" Jack called after him. "What a thing to wish on a man!"

He was still for a moment, looking after his departing friend. Then he put the cross round his neck. With me still on the saddle behind him we began to saunter along the lane as though we had not a care in the world, but I could not help being concerned about Major Grogan. If they found him in Captain Jack's coat, what would they do to him?

My father—for so I now remembered him to be—scoffed at my fears. I reminded him that Major Grogan had a bad leg. "His horse hasn't," he said. "As long as he's mounted he's good as new. Cornelius is the best roughrider I have seen. He once beat Assheton-Smith. Did you hear of him? No? Well, no matter. It means he's the best one among them. He'll run them into the ground."

Then he fell silent and I guessed he was nonplussed to remember that I now knew our relation. I was shy myself. "That's the second time you've saved my life," he said. "Here, off you get." He set me down by the roadside and then taking his foot from his stirrup, he gave me a shove with it so I fell backwards into the wet ditch.

"That's the way to treat a man who's saved your life, eh?" he said, as I emerged angry and mud-soaked. "Now they'll know you're no friend of mine. Thrown in a ditch by Captain Moonlight. Now listen, Francis. One more request. Let Lionel Bawcombe know that I'll be in the copse tonight at moonrise. Make sure you do it."

"But he may tell—"

"Make sure he *does* tell."

"You are surely not going to fight again!"

"I've a taste for it. My, it was fine in there, wasn't it? Grogan was lovely. Even Hunter Gowan was lovely; I like a man who's true to his nature! . . . You've saved me twice, Francis. I may do something for you one day. I think I'll do one thing, anyway. I shall pay you and your mother a visit. But you'll tell Lionel. *And you'll not go near that copse*. I want your promise."

"I will not promise."

"What? You shall, sir!"

"I cannot. For I cannot be sure I will keep my promise."

He stared down at me, then his anger melted as quickly as it had come. "I understand you. But if any ill befell you through me that would be the worst thing—for me. Can you understand that?"

I nodded, for I did understand him now.

"I've already used you too much. So do your *best* not to be there and do not dare interfere if the temptation's so strong that you have to be there. For my sake. For your mother's. I cannot stay to argue. But I will see you again. *I* promise that and will keep my promise."

With that he turned his horse and after a few paces began to canter in the direction of Gloucester, and left me, the chill of muddy water in my clothes and in my boots, to make my way home.

16

My Mother Learns the Truth

I left the lane at once and cut across the fields, because I did not wish to be caught up in any pursuit or asked any questions. The fewer lies I was forced to tell, the less explaining I would have to do when all this was over.

Wynne and Gowan now knew who "Captain Egerton" was: the man who had tried to shoot him, who now lay dead on the floor of the quarry, had been one of the hanging party, as had the man who ran to Sir William Wynne. It was also certain they would not rest until they found him, however far afield the disguised Major Grogan should lead them. Captain Jack had decided to let them find him, at a place of his own choosing: the copse.

What he intended to do there I could not guess. His plan so far had worked perfectly. He had publicly shown Hunter Gowan to be a cheat and a would-be murderer, and this would go far towards justifying any further fate he might have in store for him. But they would surely surround the copse, once they knew he was there, and beat through it till they found him. Of the original band of four one was dead, but with Sir William and Hunter Gowan that still made five men against one, and there might be more men at Sir William's command.

It was a desperate risk he was taking, and for a while as I crossed the fields, I raged against him. It was clear he cared for nothing except his chance and his plan. He certainly cared nothing for me, or my mother, who by now he must know lived close by. He had known who I was from the moment I had told him my name at Caleb Bawcombe's, and of my connection with Mr. Edward. At this thought I stopped below an ash tree black with the damp of the air, the moistness dripping from branch to branch as though it rained. He must have known Mr. Edward when they met on the lane before the hunt! Had Mr. Edward known him? I knew they had met once many years before, because my mother had told me. My cheeks burned as I realized that I, who thought I knew so much, had perhaps been the last to learn the secret!

Except for my mother. I thought of her and the innocent life we had lived together. It was all changed now. It was true that the bloody events of the last days—one man dead already and I feared more to die yet—were not his fault alone; but removed from his cheerful presence, standing under the cold and dismal tree, I blamed him. It was around him that all these horrible things gathered: he sought them, invited them. He did more, he *insisted* on them. I touched the tree I had known all my life, and wondered if I would ever be able to see it again as I used to, as an old friend. This morning it seemed an evil portent, weeping, slimy, boding death.

Perhaps I had come too late upon my father. I found my heart rebelling against him already. There was too much mad amusement in all he did, *and he did it for himself.*

So thinking, and disliking my fate, I came upon the Bawcombes in a field, planting a quick-set hedge and driving in a fence on each side of it, to keep off the sheep until it was well grown. Many of our wide fields were changing in this way. The common lands were being fenced into smaller sheepwalks, and there was murmuring against this, for it would mean fewer workers were needed, and some had lost their piece of tillage where they grew their food. But it was by Parliament Act, and even the fierce Bawcombes had little choice in the matter.

It was Seth I came on first, and I told him his three pieces of leather had served their purpose. "Oh yes?" he said, continuing to drive in a stake with his great hammer.

"Are you not interested?" I said, foolishly. I knew that interest was the last thing he intended to show.

"Oh yes. That's good then, isn't it?" He delivered a final blow with his hammer, picked up another stake and moved away.

"I have an important message for Lionel!" I called to his back, hating him, hating them all.

I moved down the line and Lionel straightened, putting his pale blue eyes on mine with no trace of curiosity. "Scarf Jack wants Hunter Gowan to know he will be in the copse tonight at moonrise." I felt, rather than saw,

Caleb, who was between the fences putting in the haw-
thorn cuttings, change his position the better to hear.

"Setting snares there, is he?" said Lionel, and a low
chuckle went along the line of men.

"He would particularly like it known, and wished you
particularly to carry the message."

"Oh yes?"

"Will you do it?"

"What's that then?"

"Carry the message!" Teasing was second nature with
them, as with Joel. I had shown I wanted something from
him, therefore I should not know whether I would get it.

"I might. Depends."

"Depends on what?"

He shrugged and went back to his nailing.

I stood there a moment and looked at them, all busy
with their tasks and turned from me. Then I walked
away, feeling their eyes on my back. There was no more I
could do.

It was in a black humor that I at last returned home to
my worried mother.

She had been greatly flustered by the manner of Mr.
Edward's visit. She was still in her blue dress, and a
shawl, a pretty one with a design of snowdrops on it, that
she had put on to go with him to the manor. There was
something about her best dress, and her agitation, which
put with the events of the morning and my sudden great
tiredness, made the little parlor seem unfamiliar, as
though something had happened that had changed our
lives in it. My mother moved about the room restlessly as
she spoke, hardly looking at me. "His concern made me
even more worried!" she complained. "He could not forgive himself for becoming involved in such an affair—he

told me all about it—and for involving you. He seemed to want my reassurance, but I found that difficult to give! Oh Francis, your *clothes!*" she said, looking at me properly for the first time. "What made you get in such a state?"

I told her Captain Egerton had pushed me in a ditch.

"Was that the thanks he gave you for your help? What a dreadful man! What did he do that for?" Her relief at my return had made her angry. I told her he had done it so that we should not appear particular friends, should they follow and find me, though up to that time he had been kind to me.

But her chief indignation was still against Mr. Edward. "To send you off alone at night! Get those soaking clothes off you, Francis. Why, he has barely noticed you before!" This was the first time I had heard my mother say anything against Mr. Edward, although I knew she did not warm to him. "He thinks highly of you. He told me so. But why could he not send Thomas? Because his name must not be brought into it. Though yours could be!" So she went on as I took off my wet clothes and she shook them and went into the kitchen with them, leaving me standing like a baby in the parlor with only a towel about me. "What did you find when you reached Cheltenham?" she called out, and I said, "Mother, would you mind if I dressed myself before I answer your questions?" and she said no, she did not, with a smile in her voice, for my mother's angers never lasted long.

Up in my room, dressing in dry clothes, I was glad of the opportunity to think. I resolved to answer all her questions truthfully, for I hated the idea of deceiving my mother, but to tell her nothing that she did not ask. It was perhaps wrong of me not to tell her at once that the man who had thrown me in the ditch was her husband, my father; but we had lived happily enough without him, and whatever he planned for tonight was uncertain in its outcome, and it would be cruel to raise her expectations when she might have them dashed to pieces at once by Hunter Gowan and his gang. For some reason I took it for granted she would be pleased to see my father again, and would wish to set up house with him. Though how the man I knew could set up house with any woman, or ever could have, was beyond my imagining. Perhaps he had greatly changed since they were last together.

When I was dressed I went down again to the parlor, and sat to eat some cold meat and bread my mother had put out for me, while she waited as patiently as she could, sitting before me with her elbows on the table, for the rest of my story.

"He was living in fine lodgings, shared with an old army friend who was his second in this duel. I spent the night there."

"Why did he want to fight a duel?"

"He hates Hunter Gowan, who he says did dreadful things to the people of Ireland."

"If they were rebels it was perhaps the only way."

"He said their houses were burned whether they were rebels or not, and Hunter Gowan did worse cruel things, and made the whole business in Ireland so bitter, it may take years before it is forgotten."

"I can believe it! I saw those brigands he calls his men in the manor yard . . . But *they* are Irish, so perhaps the rebels are as bad. But tell me, how did he know all this? And did his friend agree? Who was his friend?"

"He knew because he was just returned from Ireland, where he had been—helping the rebels."

"A traitor!"

"I don't think so, Mother. He just tried to protect the ordinary people from Hunter Gowan and Sir William and men like that. He said the real Army knew what he was doing, or some of it did."

"That sounds so like your father. He was always talking of the rebels in America. He had wanted to help them, but of course he could not. What was the name of Captain Egerton's friend?"

"Major Grogan."

"I knew a Grogan once. What was his Christian name?"

"Cornelius . . . I think."

My mother took her elbows off the table and pressed them to her chest, staring at me. "A sandy-colored man? Very gentle? A doctor?"

"That's him," I said, putting my face into my mug of warmed milk.

"But I knew him! Before you were born. He came back from America with your father!"

"So Hunter Gowan wanted to kill Captain Egerton because of what he knew," I went on, "and in the duel he shot Captain Egerton in the back before he had gone the agreed number of paces—"

"No!"

"And Captain Egerton fell, and everyone thought he was killed but he wasn't, because he had suspected something of the sort and had put layers of leather underneath his coat—"

"Layers of leather?" My mother's eyes were wide.

"Yes, and—"

"Your father told me he used to do that against the Indian arrows . . . I expect many soldiers did."

"And Captain Egerton got up and chased Hunter Gowan with his pistol, and caught him and looked as though he would shoot him but did not. Then he shot one of Gowan's men who was aiming at him—"

"Gracious!"

"Then he and Major Grogan rode off, Captain Egerton lifting me up with him because I was so startled by everything I could not move."

"He did that? Why should he do that?"

"I—suppose he felt I was one of his side and not one of the other side."

"And then he threw you in a ditch?"

"Yes."

"And escaped?"

"Yes."

"Leaving that Hunter Gowan alive when he had gone to such lengths to fight him? Why do you think he did not kill him?"

"I don't know. He had his pistol to his head."

"Perhaps, after all, he could not bring himself to do it," said my mother, staring at me. "Francis," she said, "could you describe Captain Egerton? How he looks? It is just possible that as a girl I may have known him."

I feared what I had to say might be too much for her, but I had promised myself I would answer her questions. "He has dark hair, short and a little curly with some gray in it. A tall-grown man, quite broad-shouldered, dark blue eyes. A thin face. Dark skin."

"Does he—wear anything strange about his person? Unusual?"

I thought of the green scarf, but I decided not to mention that because then I might have to tell the story of the

hanging and horrify my mother still further. I could think
of nothing else unusual that he wore.

"You didn't notice, when you were with him last night,
a jewel, a cross he wore beneath his clothes?"

My mother was pale. I could have told her what was
true, that last night I did not see such a cross, but I decided to deceive her no further and said yes, there had
been a cross around his neck.

"Oh, Francis, Francis! It must be." She turned to the
fire and stared into it; I could not see her face. Then she
said, "He'll be back! He'll be back for Hunter Gowan.
Oh, that dreadful man Gowan has brought death and
misery to this place as well as to Ireland. I hope your—
Captain Egerton finds him and deals with him as he de-
serves. I hope it. But that will be murder! Oh, my God!"
And she sat staring into the fire.

"He has let Hunter Gowan know he will be in the
copse on the other side of the lane tonight."

My mother gave a groan and covered her face with her
hand, then stared away again.

I was sure she wished to be by herself and I was more
than tired, as I now told her. "We were up very early. It
was all rather—tremendous. I shall sleep."

"Yes do, do, Francis," said my mother vaguely.

I stood at the door. "Did you then know Captain
Egerton?"

She looked up. "Quite well. A long time ago. Though"—
she almost smiled—"not all that well, perhaps. I—liked
him. Did you?"

"Very much."

She nodded. "Off you go, Francis. You are tired. You
have seen some horrible things."

As I climbed the stairs I was relieved to feel that for

my sake and in her turn my mother had begun to deceive
me. I was sure that the jeweled cross had told her who
Captain Egerton was, and she had decided not to tell me,
or not yet. This made me feel easier about all that I had
kept from her, for she was protecting me as—I told myself
—I had been trying to protect her. I was happy she knew
what she did, but I was indeed tired, and I was asleep in
my bed, the blankets over my head to keep out the light,
before I even had time to take off my coat and shoes, but
they were clean enough because I had only just put them
on.

17

The Fight in the Copse

I awoke dry-mouthed and muzzy in my head with no notion of how long I had slept. I knelt on my bed and looked out of the window. From the light I judged the sun was already low and that soon I must be at my place in the copse.

I could not have stayed at home. I had not promised; I had only said I would try. I tried now, and thought of sitting at home with my mother waiting until tomorrow to learn what had happened. It was impossible.

I had been right about the sun, for it soon became dusk and the evening star rose brightly above the trees. It looked as though it would be a clear night and I hoped this would favor my father.

I wondered what had happened to Hunter Gowan this morning, chasing the wrong man. My father had made me sure that Major Grogan would lead him a dance across country, so he must have returned to the village long since, baffled, to learn that Captain Jack was waiting for him in the copse!

I began to climb out of my window, to go there, but suddenly I knew those days were over. There had been something childish in all that creeping about, and I wondered if some of my father's clear-mindedness was coming to the surface in me. It was an odd feeling, to know for the first time something of the character of my own father.

I went down the stairs and passed the parlor door which stood half-open, as though my mother was listening for me and, sure enough, she called me in.

She was sitting in her high-backed chair in front of a fire that was nearly out, her chin in her hand, too deep in thought to notice how chilly the room had become. She did not look at me as I came in but said, "Where are you going?"

"I want to go to the copse, Mother, to see what will happen."

"Yes," was all she said to that. "Francis?"

"Yes, Mother?"

"Would you want to be a soldier?"

"I think not."

"Because of what you have seen?"

"Yes."

She sighed, seeming pleased, still not looking at me. "Are you not afraid to go? There may be shooting."

"A little."

"Did Captain—Egerton—ask you to be there?"

"He told me to promise not to be. I didn't promise though."

"No." She sighed again. It was nearly dark in the room now and the small light cast by the flicker of the last wood on the fire showed her face oddly calm, and smooth. I wanted to go to her and have her arms around me because it seemed dark and fierce outside, but I did not do this.

"You may be in the way, Francis. In the dark a bullet may find you and you may hamper the Captain."

"I shall try not to. He would be so angry if he saw me and he is frightening when he is angry. Also, if I distracted him he might be injured."

"If I forbade you to go, what would you do?"

"I *must* go."

"If anything happened to you it would be the end of my life, you know."

"Yes."

"Yet you will go?"

"I can't not go."

"Yes." She said it flatly, forlornly. "I have been a soldier's wife and I have had to understand." She pulled her lips back against her teeth, as though she was stopping herself crying. But when she turned to me there was a smile on her face, as though she had come to a decision. "Go now. Come back and tell me what happened. I shall sit here and try not to think of it but of happier things. Pass me my book and my spectacles, will you?"

"But the light . . ."

"Yes, I shall light the lamp in a minute. It is pleasant here in the dark."

"Shall I put something on the fire?"

"Do," she said, without interest. I did this and passed

her book and her little spectacles, both of which she left neglected on her lap.

Somewhat at a loss, for I was not used to this mood in my mother, I said good-by to her, to which she made no answer, and quitted the room and the house.

It was cold and clear outside. More stars were out and the declining evening star was very bright. At the top when I reached the lane I stopped in the shadow and looked about me. There was nothing moving except some black shapes in the field that ran and stopped and ran again and were hares.

I skirted the edge of the field in the shadow and then ran direct to the copse, making straight for the oak at the edge of it.

I reached it without being challenged and crawled inside, hardly daring to breathe until I was safe inside its darkness.

There I stayed for long moments until a small increase in light told me that the moon had at last broken clear of the trees. So now, inside my dark tree-chimney, I strained my ears for the first noise.

It was the sound of the hut door opening and of feet descending the wooden steps. I heard a man humming to himself, very contented and busy, and it was the voice of Captain Jack. Then I heard the noise of what sounded like a coil of rope being prepared and dropped on a wooden floor. After that came the crackle of twigs as my father busied himself with something in the copse. Back and forth he went, humming, then he went quiet, listening, and I saw his feet at the entrance to the oak.

I held my breath till my temples throbbed, because I remembered his extraordinary ability to hear. But he did not look inside. Instead he began to climb the tree.

I could hear him above me, settling, then he went still again and there came to my ears what he had heard so long before me, the noise of the first furtive steps into the wood, and of more than one pair of feet. Now I could hear him, very slowly and quietly, descend lower in the tree, presumably having seen all he needed.

Then, outside the tree, there was an oath and the sound of a man falling. The only knothole on this side was high for me, but I reached it somehow and saw a dark shape grabbing desperately down towards his leg. My father had been rearranging my snares along the tracks through the copse! . . . Now, past my eyes, a shape fell from the tree and threw itself on the struggling man. I saw the glint of a knife, there was a thud, a noise of choking, and I saw my father rise from the man he had stabbed just as another man came for him, before he could retrieve his knife. He fended him off with his bent arm, reached down to the ground with his other and with a swift, whipping motion clapped something over the second man's head. It was a wire snare and I remembered the look of my strangled rabbits. My arms would no longer support me at my knothole and I was not sorry. I could hear throttled gasping and Captain Jack saying, "Have you had enough? Will you run? Will you not come back? Will you remember your life was spared when next you have a man's life in your hands? Will you? Will you?"

He must have been twisting the wire and then he must have let go because I heard the man gagging for breath and after this there was a noise as though my father had sent him sprawling. I heard him say, "Begone, or by God!" and it seemed the man did not need to be told again for I heard him gasping and spitting and tearing through brambles, then the drum of his feet on the turf outside as he made off.

At this point there was more movement in the undergrowth and a voice whispered hoarsely, "You all right, Captain?" and Captain Jack swore in the darkness. "Caleb! What the devil are you doing here? Get out of it, man!" Then I heard Caleb call aloud, "Oho! Interfere with my snares, would you?" and there was now a crashing that terrified me, for it seemed possible that Caleb had turned on my father. "You know what we do with the likes of you in these parts, do you? We toss 'em in the river and that's just where you're going, my beauty!" Desperately I crawled to the hole at the bottom of the oak and put out my head. Caleb held in his arms a kicking figure, but it was not my father, his shape I could see to one side. It was the third of Gowan's men that Caleb held now high above his head so that all his cursing and kicking was to no avail. It was in this fashion that Caleb bore him, like a naughty child, out of the copse and towards the river.

My father had seen me now and grasped me by my collar, hauling me out from the tree so roughly that the skin was taken from my sides. "What, in God's name! . . . I thought I made you promise! Get over there, boy!" he said, hurling me in my turn into the briars behind him. "And *stay* there! I don't want infants and villagers getting in the way, d'you hear!" He was angry, and panting, so I lay where I was and said nothing, though it was exceedingly painful.

Ignoring me he pushed his way to the hut, returning with the coil of rope. Putting his arm through it he began to climb the tree. From there he hissed, "If you so much as dare to move . . ." with such venom that I would have been incapable of movement if the bush had indeed been composed of nails, as it felt, instead of thorns.

Once up the tree he sat still, waiting, and he did not have to wait for long.

After maybe five minutes there came a voice from the slope of the field above the copse. "Quillen? . . . Boylan? . . . Keogh? . . ." Even at a whisper Gowan's voice was harsh. It was possible he had not seen the fate of two of his men who still lived, for each, one in the arms of Caleb, had left the copse by the bottom end, out of his view, but he must have heard the sounds of struggle. The absence of reply must have told the story and it says much for his courage that he now entered the wood himself.

He had a pistol in each hand and moved slowly, testing his foot on the ground before he put his weight on it, glancing round at every step and up into the trees. He approached the oak and stared carefully up but appeared to see nothing. I could see nothing there either, but some of the boughs were so thick it would be just possible for a man to lie full-stretch and his shape to be concealed.

If Captain Jack did not act soon, Gowan was sure to come upon me as I lay among the briars. I had turned my face down into the bush so that the white of it would not catch his eye, but it was almost bright in the copse by now and I watched him sideways, very fearful.

I saw his dark shape stoop and half kneel as he found his confederate lying dead. I wondered if it was the leader, Quillen, with the black eyebrows. Then he stood and called out softly, as though this was a private affair in a private room, "I know you are here. Come out." It was this moment Captain Jack chose to make his leap.

He must have been lying on one of the boughs directly above his enemy, for he simply fell on him, stretched out

like a planing bird, and landed on Gowan with a dreadful
sound, bearing them both to the ground.

If Gowan was stunned he showed no sign of it; bunch-
ing himself up with a sort of grunt he hurled Jack from
him and pulled himself to his feet and crouched, facing
him. Jack had the rope ready and as Gowan came for him
he slipped the noose over his head and drew it tight with
a jerk that snapped back Gowan's head and brought him
to his knees. On the ground he scrabbled with his hand
for one of his dropped pistols and Captain Jack brought
his heel down hard on his outstretched hand so that
Gowan yelped.

Of all the things that happened that night I remembered best the ease and force with which my father was
able to stamp on Gowan's hand. They were fighting for
their lives but I feared him then and hated the whole
bloody business. You may ask what else would I have him
do? Allow Gowan the use of his pistol? Perhaps I was better able to imagine the pain of a crushed hand than I was
to imagine death by stabbing. All I know is that I sensed
a relish in it.

He picked up the pistol himself with his right hand,
holding it to Gowan's head, with his other at Gowan's
throat, some of the rope wound round his fist and the
noose held tight. He pulled Gowan out of the copse to the
field side of the tree from which he had been left to hang.

His purpose was clear and I had no wish to see it
carried out. Bleeding from my face and hands I pulled
myself out of the briars and made for the edge of the
copse. I wanted to be in the open where I could breathe.
I felt as stifled as Gowan who, through all these proceed-
ings, had made no sound.

But leave the field I could not. I tried, but I was unable. Fixed and frozen as in a dream I stood at the edge of the copse with the bright moon and the bright stars over my head. I saw my father hurl the loose end of the rope over a bough, retrieve it, and pull on it till Gowan stood on the tips of his shoes, nearly suspended.

I heard him say, breathing heavily, "What did they call that big sergeant? Tom the Devil? The one who hanged men over his shoulder and let them strangle behind him as he walked? I saw that. You had good sport, didn't you, Hunter Gowan? I'm not so tall as the sergeant, or you are too long. Soon you'll be longer!" He pulled on the rope and Gowan left the ground, dreadfully kicking his feet to retain contact with it.

Then my father stopped pulling, Gowan hung there, and my father gave a noise like a groan, let go the rope altogether and Gowan fell to the turf at the edge of the copse.

My father cried out, beside himself, "Fight, damn you! Fight! Fight!" and began tearing the noose from Gowan's neck. When he had it off he fell back and knelt, panting, staring at his enemy, who was also on his knees taking great gulps of air with his tongue hanging out of his mouth like a dog's.

I do not know how long the two men stayed there in this way in the moonlight in perfect hatred. It was as though they made a world between them and nothing else existed. Then Gowan sprang forward and they rolled over and over, like badgers, snarling, groaning, biting, first one on top and then the other, dreadful squelching blows being exchanged but I could not tell by whom or on whom, so closely were they intertwined; they seemed like one man in torment.

I knew that I should help my father but I could not. I

knew that I should get no thanks but that is not what stopped me. It was this sense of a private world shared by these two men who had now become animals, with only one idea: to kill each other.

Then came a great shout, unmistakably from my father, and I saw him arch up in agony, almost detached from Gowan, but not quite. Gowan had his teeth fixed in my father's leg just above the knee.

It was a game we played in the schoolroom, pinching each other just above the kneecap. If you found the right place it was impossible not to make your victim jump and kick the desk, causing Mr. Turner to look up and frown. If pressure of finger and thumb could cause such an uncontrollable reaction, it was easy to understand that my father was for that moment helpless.

The moment was long enough. Gowan released his bite and fell on my father to make an end of the business, by strangling him.

I do not know if it was fear that made me unable to move. Certainly it seemed my father was spent and if I went to his aid I would have to face Hunter Gowan alone. But I like to think it was not fear that held me back, that I would have gone to my father's assistance had not a high voice called from inside the copse, "Stop, sir. Stop at once or I fire!"

Gowan continued his throttling, now having hold of my father's scarf, lying sideways across him and extending his arms to get better purchase.

"Stop!" came the voice in an imploring screech, then there was a shot and Gowan paused as though surprised at the noise but he did not look round. He fell sideways to the turf and lay still.

From the copse stepped Mr. Edward, smoke coming

from the muzzle of his rifle, the beautiful one with the walnut stock that had designs pressed into it with silver wire.

His face looked yellow in the moonlight and his eyes were staring.

"I could do nothing else," he said, in a high, strange voice. "I could not see murder done. I came down to stop it . . . I heard." He walked towards my father as though he barely saw him. "I could do nothing else."

My father recovered himself slowly, feeling his neck, putting his head between his knees.

"I warned him. I warned him twice," said Mr. Edward, standing over my father and the body of Gowan but looking at neither.

My father was groaning, rocking himself to and fro. "God help Ireland!" He sounded in despair. "We cannot hate for our country—we *have* no country! D'you see?"

"Sir William must take the—body—away," said Mr. Edward. "And the other body. He gave assurances . . ." His voice trailed away.

"Gowan could hate from fear. Property makes men devils, fear of the loss of it. But the poor Irish *have* no property, have no country. So how can we hate, as he does? Unless England binds us together in hatred, *then* we'll kill for Ireland—for a name—God help us!" Tears were running down my father's face. "I wanted to kill that bloody man for *myself*, not for Ireland. I couldn't do it—not in cold blood. *I could not do it!*" He was twisting his hands together as though he would break his fingers; he seemed in mental agony. "Must we then always lose, unless we hate? Must a poor man hate, in order to live at all?" He addressed the questions to the air but turned his face beseechingly up to Mr. Edward as though desperate for an answer from anyone.

But Mr. Edward, still like one in a dream, continued his own thoughts. "Trespassing on my property," he said in a strange flat voice. "Failed to answer my challenge. I fired."

"You saved my life, Mr. Edward!" My father made an effort to collect himself, seeing the condition of the other man, and spoke more loudly, as though to rouse a sleepwalker. From his sitting position he stared up at his deliverer. The moon made the tears on my father's cheeks glitter, and the tears that stood in his eyes. Mr. Edward moved his own eyes slowly downward and said, still with hardly any expression in his voice, "I know you."

"You are not well," said my father, falling forward on his knees and, with the help of his hand, pushing himself up slowly until he stood, facing Mr. Edward.

Mr. Edward's eyes avoided his and turned slowly to where I stood. "The boy. You must see his mother. You will be leaving the neighborhood. Of course. I must be gone. I must send—I must send down for Captain Gowan. I must—I do not," he held a hand to his head, "know how best to proceed."

"You had best sit down," said my father, laying a hand on his arm. Mr. Edward drew away quickly, as though coming to himself.

"It will be understood," he said, "I dare say. Defense of property. But a death . . . You must go and visit your wife, sir," he suddenly commanded. "With your son."

"You saw the end of me tonight, Francis," said my father, with an attempt at cheerfulness, but his voice caught in his throat. "I'm used up. I couldn't do it. Not any more." He took a few paces and staggered, falling to one knee.

"Take him to your cottage. To your mother. Tell her—yes, tell your mother how it occurred . . . the end of Gowan."

I knelt on the ground and tried to support my father as Mr. Edward left us. He slowly crossed the field with his gun held away from his side, as though it was something dirty that did not belong to him.

My father fell from my arm and lay on the grass with his face sideways, his eyes open, as though he had given up entirely. I sat him up as well as I could, putting my arm about him again, and he seemed exhausted, utterly in despair with himself. He was heavy to hold up and over his shoulder I saw Mr. Edward continue in a straight line across the field and on to the lane, his gun still held away from him; then he was lost to sight. Hunter Gowan lay where he had fallen, at the edge of the copse under the oak tree, more still than a man asleep, more still than I had imagined possible, with his face turned up to the moon.

18

The End of the Adventure

We did not stay like this for long; I felt after a few moments that my father ceased to give me his full weight. Then he gathered himself and pulled away, looking at me with his head back. "My horse," he said. "I have it at the field's edge. Over there."

He stood up, easily enough, but with a grunt. He reached his hand down for me to grasp and as he pulled me to my feet I was surprised at the roughness and hardness of his palm.

We walked in silence to the trees that bordered the field. There was an awkwardness between us and I wondered if my father's moments of weakness would make him shy of me, or resentful.

"I leave Mr. Edward in some difficulty," he said. "Ah well."

He said no more and when we reached the wood I ventured a question that troubled me, though I was nervous to ask it. "Is he—dead? The man you stabbed?"

"Quillen was a great rogue," said my father curtly. After a long pause he added, as though answering my thought, "I do not enjoy it, Francis. Nor am I good at it. As you saw."

We found his horse in a clearing, waiting patiently, and my father made much of him, soothing him, whispering to him, and led him out into the field. When we were out in the open I asked if he were not afraid to be followed and he said he was not. "There are none left, not here anyway. Sir William won't stir till the morning."

"Where will you go now?"

"With you."

"My mother—may be a little startled."

"Do you not know her? She could make two of the both of us."

There was time for me to work this out because my father spoke no more as we crossed the field in full view. I took him to mean that my mother was twice the men we were, so to say, and I liked him for saying that. When we reached the lane the echo of the iron hooves made me flinch and look about me, but my father was untroubled.

At last we reached the safety of the trees above our cottage and when my father saw the steps cut in the bank he turned his horse aside to the woodshed, tethering it there facing outwards. I saw how careful he was. He measured the distance from the shed to the lane with his eye, cocking his head to do so, as he talked softly to the horse again, smoothing its nose.

He went slowly down the steps, lagging behind me. "Francis," he whispered, "have you a spring nearby, or a trough? I am thirsty and I should like to throw some water over my face. In a few moments I shall need all my wits about me." There was something in his voice that made me turn and I thought I saw him smiling at me.

I led him to the spring under the yew tree and he knelt at the side of it, cupping water in his hands and drinking, then scooping handfuls over his face and head. Gasping, he stood up, smoothing his hair and clothes.

"Shall I go in and warn her?" I said.

"Have you told her anything of the strange man you met?"

"A little."

"Enough?"

"I think so."

"We shall go in together."

Again I led him, this time round the side of the cottage to the door. He paused for a moment, taking a breath, then we went in. I called out, "Mother? I have brought someone to see you," and I heard her rise from her chair. My father stepped past me into the room.

My mother was standing with an expression on her face I had never seen before. It was more like no expression at all, very calm and controlled. My father said, "May I come in for a moment, Jane?"

"Of course," said my mother, not moving. "You are wounded?"

"Not a bit of it."

"You are pale, Jack."

"And you look well," said my father quietly. "Very well."

"Are you pursued?"

"I think not."

"Then you must sit down."

"Thank you."

"Francis, your face is bleeding."

"I fell in a bramble bush in the dark."

My mother turned her attention back to my father, seating herself opposite him. "Does Francis . . . ?"

"Now he does," said my father, but seeing an expression of pain pass over her face because I had kept my knowledge from her—the first expression of any kind that she had shown—he added quickly, "But he has not known long enough to be able to tell you. The whole thing is the strangest chance, with Sir William Wynne at the bottom of it."

My mother nodded, as though impatient. "You are the man they are looking for?"

"Yes."

"Oh, *Jack!*"

"It's a long story, Jane."

"Fourteen years," said my mother and my father looked away. "Are you hungry?" she said.

"I am."

"I'll get you something. Francis, come and help me." I felt my mother did not want me to be alone with him, for in the kitchen she had nothing for me to do, and she found meat and bread for him and a tumbler of brandy from a bottle I did not know we possessed. She bade me find some food for myself as she took a tray in to my father.

When I returned to the parlor, as quickly as I could, the food had already disappeared and my father had his face in the tumbler, drinking deep, looking at my mother over the rim of it as though teasing her. She returned his look, neither smiling nor unsmiling, as though observing, the way I have seen women look at each other's clothes, or as people watch an actor in a play. My father put the tumbler aside with a sigh, carefully wiping his mouth with a handkerchief. He looked round the parlor.

"Fourteen years," he said. "I left you in wider circumstances."

My mother told him of the unlucky business ventures of her father, of his death, and of the help given to us both by Mr. Edward. Seeing my father look round the room again at the mention of Mr. Edward, she added, "He has many calls on his purse," and my father said nothing.

"And you, Jack?" she asked.

"It is too long, Jane. I never wrote, for reasons I know you will understand. Now I should have to start from the beginning. It would take too long."

"Your coat does not fit well."

My father smiled. "It is Con Grogan's. Remember him?" Then, as though reminded by his friend's name, "See? I still have it"; and he fumbled at his coat and shirt until, bending forward, he pulled out the jeweled cross. "I've never parted with it," he said, turning wide eyes on me so that, despite myself, I could hardly help laughing. Then he returned the cross to his bosom, giving himself a small shake to settle it and letting out a little involuntary cry as he did so.

"You *are* wounded, Jack!" said my mother, alarmed.

"Not at all, a bruise only."

"Let me see. I insist. You do not look well."

"No, Jane."

"I would do it for a poor man who came to the door. I should like to see, Jack."

"What you see you will not like."

"How do you know, now, what I like and what I do not!"

My father looked seriously at my mother for a moment, stood up and took off his coat. Then, pulling off his shirt impatiently, keeping the scarf still about his neck, he half turned his back towards her. She gave a gasp when she saw the whipping scars and said, "Jack! What have you been doing to yourself!"

My father grunted with amusement. "You put it well. I sometimes wonder. But that's old. Could you bear to look closer and see—there's an ache that troubles me."

My mother stepped to look closer and so did I. There was a spreading bruise to the left of my father's spine, just below the shoulder blade. My mother drew in her breath, then she saw me and said, "Francis, I think you should go to bed."

"Let him stay. I mean—could the boy not stay a little, Jane? He's seen much. He saw this happen."

"You turned your back and let Hunter Gowan aim at your heart!"

"I was not *sure* he would do it, Jane. But I was glad he didn't shoot low."

"I will get some grease. Where is that dreadful Gowan now?" she called as she went busily to the kitchen. I could see she was glad to have something to do. "He is in the field," said my father, looking at me.

My mother, returning quickly with some goose grease, a towel and a kettle which she put on the fire, said, "In the field?"

"He'll be there till somebody moves him, Jane."

She paused for a moment with her hand on the kettle, her back to us, and said, "You killed him."

"No."

She turned, "Who, then?"

My father look at me again. "Mr. Edward."

She gave an exclamation of real horror and rounded furiously on my father. "You have brought murder and sorrow on us! What is the poor man to do now, with a death on his hands! He is not used to it, like you!"

My father answered with his eyes closed, sitting astride a wooden chair, his back to her. "I don't know," and he winced as she put the first of the grease on his back, none too gently. "I know I did not intend to bring murder to you. I did not intend to visit you at all!" He craned his neck round to her, venturing a smile. The movement slightly disarranged his scarf and my mother cried, "Your neck!"

"For God's sake, Jane. You're a soldier's wife. Wounds don't make you squeal. Ease my bruise if you can and if you want; if not, have done. All that you want to know I shall tell you."

This speech, firmly, even roughly delivered, as though there was still some understanding between my mother and father, seemed to calm her and she continued applying the grease and rubbing it in with her fingers, but more gently than at first.

"Well," she said, "what are you doing here if not to visit me?"

"I did not even know you were here or where I was. It is the purest good fortune—ouch!—that I find myself with you. I was helping out in Ireland. It became too dangerous." My father looked at his empty glass and my mother went out to replenish it. After she had done so she said, "And?"

"His men brought me where they knew he was expected and tried to hang me. It was raining. Too wet for them. Francis cut me down."

My mother turned to me, flushed. My father was watching out of the corner of his eye and said, "Of course he didn't tell you! It might have been dangerous. He's a brave boy."

"What good have you ever done him?"

"That's only your anger talking."

The kettle was now bubbling on the fire and my mother went to it, soaking the towel in hot water so that it steamed. She put the hot towel to my father's back and he bared his teeth.

"Too hot?"

"No, it's good."

"A soldier's wife . . . I was once. But you are not a soldier. You left the Army. I heard that."

"Soldiers are always on the wrong side."

"So I remember you saying," said my mother, grim.

"It's half true, anyway," said my father, grinning. "May I turn?"

"I think it's enough. The best I can do. You must rest. Finish your brandy."

My father sat up, adjusted his scarf and pulled his shirt back on. Then he took a deep drink and pronounced that he felt better already. My mother filled his glass again and he smiled his thanks. "Soldiering was all I knew. Fighting, anyway."

"All the time since I last saw you?"

"No, I tried farming. In Ireland. In America. I liked it. But it seems that fighting is what I go back to."

"And finish with a back like that?"

"Am I finished? Maybe I am."

My mother regarded him for a moment and then asked, gently, "Will you stay here?"

"With you? And Francis?"

"I have to ask it."

"Do you expect me to?"

"No."

"Do you *want* me to, for God's sake?"

"That would depend. On a lot of things."

"Of course it would! It's not refusing you, Jane, or Francis. You know that. It's the kind of man I am. It takes years to learn." For my father this was a humble speech.

My mother was silent. I could not help noticing they understood one another and agreed about many things, but that my mother was always slightly attacking my father. "Would you want Francis to be a soldier?"

"You know the answer to that!"

"I would like Francis to hear you give it."

"Men only become soldiers because they're poor or stupid. Or have no imaginations. They want to find out if they're brave. I did. Think of it! Some of the bravest men in a battle have no other human quality whatever!"

"You have had many friends who are soldiers, Jack," said my mother.

"I know it, Jane," said my father, humble again. "I talk."

"Major Grogan said something like that to me," I said.

"Like what?" asked my father.

"That it takes more bravery to live than to die."

"Did he, by God! I can guess when he said it, too. And he's right . . . He's here in the town, Jane. You should go and visit him."

"Why? Do you think we are lonely?"

"Not at all. It was only an idea. You must do as you please."

"Thank you," said my mother, with a little, mocking inclination of her head. "My old maid's life suits me well. So, Ireland is where you have been. That country was always in your blood. Like a poison."

"Why do you add that, Jane? Poison?" My father stood up and reached for Major Grogan's coat, forcing his arms into it. "Have you told Francis about his grandfather, my father?" He turned to me. "He was a clergyman, Francis. Of the Church of Ireland. Has your mother told you? The Church of Ireland! There was not a poor man for a hundred miles around who didn't belong to another church altogether, the Catholic church, and he hadn't even a church building, his priests had to lurk in ditches. He hadn't much of anything else either. What do you make of that? Poison? Where did the poison come from? My father had little enough money and he spent it all trying to make an English gentleman out of me—not an Irish gentleman, mind you. I doubt if he knew one existed. He bought me my commission . . . I did my best to please him, till he died. But in the end I felt more at home with those poor people. No, Jane, I'm not ashamed of what I've been doing. Not until these last few days, anyway. All these theatricals, in front of my son. They don't pass in England, somehow. Safe, steady England. Mr. Edward and his regular ways . . . Poor fellow!" He said it without much feeling, almost with a chuckle. "No, I'm not ashamed of what I've done—and may do yet."

"You speak in a more Irish fashion than when I knew you," said my mother.

"We discover who we are and then we play the part. Like actors. Don't we, Jane? You'll never believe this in

England, yet you're the biggest actors of the world. Mr. Edward thinks he's a country gentleman whereas all the time he merely behaves as he thinks befits one. He's an actor. You are a lady. In an old shawl and your hair hanging down in wisps, would you still feel a lady? Would you be one? Me, with my shoulders whipped on the triangle, did I not feel a peasant? Was I not one at that moment? If I now choose to play the highwayman, is that not what I am?"

"You enjoy it!"

"A reason for not doing it? Hush! What's that?"

My father stood quite still and we all strained to listen. Then we heard the noise. It was the bough of an elder tree scraping the roof and we told him so.

"Are you sure you're not followed, Jack?"

"Nothing is sure. I am tired, though. Would you hide me?"

"Yes."

"Thank you. I shall be gone before dawn."

"So soon?"

My father smiled. "Soon enough, I think. Francis, you must get some rest too, for I must talk a little with your mother."

A glance from my mother showed me that she would like to be alone with my father, so I went upstairs reluctantly, though I was more than tired.

I heard my mother ask him where he would go and he again said France or America, so I thought I should perhaps never see him again. But it was true that he did not fit into our lives. I could not imagine him living with us. Though I had sensed that he and my mother, in a different sort of world, might have gone campaigning together.

As I undressed for bed I heard my father say, "That is a fine boy, Jane. You have done well," and my mother shushed him because she knew that I could overhear. After that their voices dropped to a murmur, my father's causing a sort of small shaking in the walls, like a bass viol, so that I could hear it when I could not distinguish the words, or know whether my mother replied or not. They sounded private together.

This was the first time I had fallen asleep with a man's voice in our house making that odd booming sound and I remember thinking that I loved and admired my father, was glad at last to have met him, but I was not sorry he would not stay forever because it would make my life so very different.

I must have been determined to catch one more sight of him because I sleep soundly, but I woke to find him standing in my doorway. He came to my bed and stood over me and I kept my eyes shut. He touched my forehead with his fingers, then went quietly out of the room. I heard him in the hall pulling on his coat, then I heard the door close softly behind him and his feet on the path outside my window.

I jumped out of bed, pulled on my coat and boots and followed him outside. It was still dark, perhaps half an hour before dawn, but I saw his shape halfway up the steps in the bank. I ran after him, my unlaced boots making a flapping noise, and he turned and stopped.

"Have you come to see me off? That is good of you," he said softly when I reached him. He put his arm round my shoulders. It was awkward; we each had to walk at the side of the narrow steps in order to stay together, but he did not take his arm away.

He found his horse and tightened the girth. When he

had climbed into the saddle he looked down at me, pondering. "I should give you something, Francis. A father should." He thought for a moment and delved inside Major Grogan's coat for the cross, pulling it over his neck. He held it in his palm, looking at it and looking at me. Then he laughed, put the string over his head again and buttoned his coat. "I may need it. Who knows? The trick is, Francis—to give up killing but not be killed yourself." He patted the cross under his coat and spoke with such impudence that dearly as I would have loved the cross I could not help laughing and he began to laugh quietly himself. Then he grew more grave, but not much more, and said, "Look after your mother, but I don't need to say that. Will you take a look at the road and see if it's clear?"

I walked a few paces to the lane and stood above the copse where we had met. It was too dark to see if Hunter Gowan still lay there. It was too dark to see anything but I listened and all was very still. A cock crowed in the village at the bottom of the field. People would soon be stirring. I waved my father out of the trees and onto the road. He leaned down and took my hand briefly. Then he let it go and rode into the dark.

That is the end of the story of Scarf Jack, or at least of my part in it. When I returned to the cottage I found my mother at the bottom of the stairs. I saw her face by the light of her candle and I was struck by the strength in it, as much as there was in my father's. I have never forgotten that glimpse I had of her, or the way she turned without a word and went back to her room.

There is little to add, except that Ireland was pacified, more or less. But I fear the wounds of that unhappy country are not so easy to heal. Because of those days and what I learned from my father, I have never been able to believe that these pains and sorrows are wholly the fault of the Irish Catholics themselves, as many of my neighbors continue to believe.

After my father was gone Mr. Edward appeared much less certain of this also. He seemed much less certain of everything, as though his stiff nature had been softened by the shocks he had received. What became of the body of Hunter Gowan, of the man my father killed in the copse and the one he killed in the quarry, I never discovered. It was not a matter that we ever referred to again. They were not there when I looked next day. Perhaps Sir William Wynne was as good as his word and spirited them away in order to hide his part in the business. Certainly that gentleman was seen no more, either. Or perhaps Mr. Edward had them secretly buried. He was more considerate to me and to my mother, to the Bawcombes and to all his tenants. So perhaps the terrible events in Ireland which spilled so briefly into our part of Gloucestershire had some good effect after all.

Within two years of my father's departure I moved with my mother into the town. After a short while there, showing some signs of my father's restlessness—or so my mother told me—and remembering her advice not to marry until I had worked some of it out of my system, I took myself to sea. There, with Major Grogan's help, I became in due course a ship's surgeon. This has given me a life with adventures enough in it but not perhaps so many as were in my father's. Nor would I wish for as many, but I have had my share.

My mother and Major Grogan became fast friends, as my father had hoped. When on leave from the Service I have spent many contented evenings with both of them

together. Since his appearance and disappearance my
mother has been able to talk much more easily about the
man she married, and I know she admires him very
much, though regarding the way he lives as quite impossible.

As for myself I have not been able to make up my mind
about him. I think of his hand outlined against the river. I
feel again the roughness of his palm as he helped me to
my feet; I remember his sudden hilarities, his equally
quick angers; a sense of play-acting about all he did, although his life was on the hazard. He was a strange man.

He is still. On one of my rides up to Elstone I came
across old Caleb. He was smoking a fine meerschaum pipe
with a silver band. He showed it to me, and on the band
was written, in fine copperplate, *From his fellow poacher
Scarf Jack*. He told me it arrived one day from foreign
parts, with no address attached. He cannot remember
from where.

Sometimes on my journeys I hear tales of a man who
does not sound unlike him. Perhaps we shall meet again.